Tricks

by

Margaret Gregory

Tried and Trusted Indie Publishing

Tricks

Cover designed by Mardragon
Cover Image Credits: © Can Stock Photo Inc. /racorn
© Can Stock Photo Inc. / ISerg

Also by Margaret Gregory
TYMOREAN TRUST SERIES:
Book 1 - Power Rising
Book 2 - Great Ones
Book 3 - The Return to Earth
Book 4 – Earth Mission
Book 5 – Alien Contact
Book 6 - Invasion
ATAPI SORCERESS SERIES:
Prequel – Korvu: The Beginning
Book 1- The Wild One
Book 2 – Atapi Sorceress
THE THIRD GENERATION SERIES:
Wanda: From Bad to Worse
Wanda: Choosing Crime
Wanda – Early Days (anthology) Book 1 and 2
Wanda – Risking Life to Live

For permission requests, address the request to the author c/o:
triedandtrustedindie@gmail.com

Printed in Australia

Publisher of record
Tried and Trusted Indie Publishing
www.tatindiepublishing.com.au

Tricks

Chapter 1

The classroom door slammed shut.

For a moment, nobody moved. Then, one by one, every member of the class was overcome and helpless with laughter. The history lesson had been tedious. Seemingly endless notes to be written down, dictated in a monotone drone. The slides projected on the over-the-board screen were totally devoid of interest.

Without warning, the projector screen had fallen off the wall. Everyone was startled, including the teacher, Mrs Burgess. However it was the poster, hidden until then by the screen, which now had everyone laughing.

The poster itself had been on the black board for over a week, but someone had since modified it. Now there was a figure of a person in a very undignified position, (cut out from a blown up photo) stuck onto the poster, turning the dreary picture into a masterpiece of comic humour.

The only person close enough to identify the person in the photo was the teacher, and she recognised herself.

It was no wonder that the normally prim and dignified teacher had walked out. She had not known that she had been photographed when she had slipped on the oval during the previous week at the annual sports day.

Tom Dwyer and his sister Jo were laughing so hard they were almost gasping for breath. Yet it didn't stop them from quickly winding up the almost invisible pieces of nylon fishing line that had caused the screen to fall down in the first place. Finally, Tom felt the hook that he had loosened come into his hand.

"I suppose we should see if we can put the screen back up," Tom suggested to Steve Reynolds who was across the table from him.

Steve, the class captain of Ten Silver pushed himself to his feet, still laughing.

"Come on then!"

While Reynolds struggled with the screen, helped by Jo Dwyer, Tom pretended to be hunting for the hook.

"Here's the hook," he said after bending down and appearing to pick it up.

Steve was up on a chair when the Deputy Principal, Marcus Hendry, entered the room.

He walked to the poster and removed the cut out photo from it.

"What happened here?" he asked without preamble, and seeming to look at everyone in the class.

The laughter died immediately and everyone now looked seriously innocent.

Hendry switched his gaze to the three at the front.

"Reynolds?"

"The screen fell down, Sir," Steve said honestly. "Tom and I were trying to see if we could put it back up."

"And this photo?" he asked without a trace of mirth.

Jo answered that. "It wasn't there this morning at homeroom."

That statement was true enough and she managed to sound perplexed.

Tom Dwyer turned his face away until he could control his expression. He'd placed the photo there and pulled the screen down to hide it, during the confusion of everyone leaving the homeroom that morning. He knew that room was not used between then and the time of their history class on a Monday morning.

Their homeroom teacher had not noticed and Mrs Burgess had simply thought that someone had been kind enough to pull the screen down for her.

Hendry looked thoughtfully at the Dwyer siblings, but kept his thoughts to himself when he addressed the class as a group.

"I don't believe this was an accident," he said directly. "The person or people responsible are expected to apologise to Mrs Burgess."

His eyes swept over the seated students, none of whom was game to move their head in any way to indicate a response to the request. He met Tom Dwyer's gaze, noted the faint twitch of his mouth and the relief in his expression when the bell rang for lunch.

With a shrug and a sideways nod of his head, Hendry allowed the class to leave.

"Leave the screen, Reynolds. I'll have the maintenance man fix it."

Tom and Jo Dwyer were full of inner mirth for the rest of the day. They had one more trick planned and that was intended for homeroom that afternoon.

All of the students of Ten Silver were listening to the notices being read by their homeroom teacher, Devin Rhodes. Twenty-six pairs of eyes were watching the clock behind him, ready to spring up when the final bell rang.

Tom gave a sideways glance at his sister. For the second time that day, an unexpected clatter made everyone jump. The cupboard at the back of the room flew open and a shelf of books and papers slid out onto the floor. Students twitched, glancing to look at what had fallen.

Rhodes continued reading his list of notices as if nothing had happened. However, now, he began to walk around the room, not noticeably looking at any student. As if by chance, he was standing next to Jo Dwyer as the final bell rang.

"Tom, since you and your sister were so helpful earlier, perhaps you'd like to offer to help clean up the mess and reset the shelves."

Tom looked up at the teacher, expressionless and said, "Okay, that's fine, we can do that."

Steve Reynolds had paused for a moment, wondering if he was meant to help too, but hoping he didn't have to. Rhodes did not glance his way or say anything further, so he raced out to basketball practice.

Rhodes maintained his position as the last of the other students left the room. Most of them would suspect that the Dwyer siblings were to be given a reprimand – again, though they had been behaving themselves for the past few weeks.

"I thought that you had both put an end to your juvenile pranks."

Rhodes's voice was quiet but hard.

"Why are you blaming us," Tom challenged, also quietly, acting innocent.

"It was particularly noticeable, that when the cupboard fell open, only two people in the room didn't jump and turn around to see what the noise was."

Tom continued to stare back at his teacher.

"It was equally obvious, that at least one of those two was fiddling with something under the table."

Rhodes suddenly leant down and grabbed the fishing line that Tom had not been able to finish reeling in. He pulled it until all the line was in his hand. Including the end that had a pencil tied to it.

"I'm sure I could find something similar in Jo's pocket. I presume you sabotaged the projector screen in a similar way."

Rhodes met Jo's eyes and she dropped hers first.

"I will not tolerate disrespect for your teachers or towards myself."

"It was a harmless joke," Jo said, not quite resentfully. "History is boring."

"That is no reason to cause profound embarrassment to a member of staff – one who works hard to teach her students and who genuinely wants to help them do well."

"Well, she can help everyone else!" Tom blurted. "She doesn't have to keep on our case."

"Perhaps if you worked harder in all your classes, your teachers would leave you alone. Don't you want to do well?"

"We do well enough," Tom argued.

"If you deigned to finish your homework and assignments on time, you'd find things different."

Tom simply shrugged, a gesture copied by his sister. Rhodes refrained from sighing.

"Very well, let me give you a warning. Continue as you have today and you will be sent home."

Jo looked startled, Tom's expression hardened.

"Wouldn't bother me," Tom said. "We'd be on our own all day."

Rhodes did not react to Tom's assertion, but he filed it away in his memory.

"When you have finished putting the cupboard to rights, you can go home. That means that if you have a bus to catch, you'd better hurry."

"We walk," Jo muttered, rising from her seat.

Rhodes went back to his desk and allowed Tom to join his sister.

He studied them while they worked. Neither spoke, but they worked diligently. He could find no fault with the finished chore. It surprised him. He had expected sullenness and a tendency to throw things back in the cupboard, or to slam things down and at best an indifferent job. Perhaps they had decided to heed his warning.

After taking as long as they dared to fix up the cupboard, Tom and Jo grabbed their bags and Rhodes allowed them to go home.

For the first quarter of an hour, as they walked home, Tom hummed a discordant tune and Jo plodded in silence.

"You don't really think they will suspend us," Jo finally spoke what was on her mind.

"They'd better not," Tom muttered. "We're only playing harmless pranks for heaven's sake. He was just trying to frighten us."

"Well he succeeded," Jo admitted. "The last thing I want is to have to stay at home when Uncle's around."

"Yeah, last time they just gave us detention."

"Well with luck, Uncle will have left for work by the time we get home today," Jo hoped. "Trust Rhodes to spoil my good mood."

"Well," Tom smiled. "I still think Burgess got what she deserved."

Jo grinned, but half-heartedly.

They walked in silence until they reached home.

Chapter 2

Home, was a shabby looking two storey house in amongst a row of similar dwellings. Theirs had no garden, just scrubby grass that needed cutting and a cement path from the gate to the door. Neither Tom nor Jo had any wish to invite friends there. Then again, they were seldom allowed to visit their friends' homes either.

On that afternoon, to one side of the path was an untidy pile of briquettes, the hard coal lumps that were used in the lounge room enclosed fire place. They needed to skirt it to reach the unmade path down the side of the house. It was just wide enough to walk single file between house and fence so they could go inside, entering via the back door, to which they both had keys. Today it was already unlocked so they entered quietly so as not to disturb their Aunt who was moving around in the kitchen. They had seen the briquettes on the front lawn but were in no hurry to move them.

"The briquettes were delivered today. Could you bring them around the back for me?" Hilda Dwyer asked them. She sounded distracted.

"Sure Aunt Hilda," Jo agreed. "We'll do it in a mo'."

They continued upstairs to drop their school bags and change out of their school uniforms. Jo's idea of a mo', was that they would do it eventually; she wanted to watch a show on TV. Tom wanted a snack first.

However as they went past their Uncle's room, the one nearest the top of the stairs, the door opened and he stepped out. Edward Dwyer was not a tall man but he was solid. He had a lot of chest hair, only some of which was showing from under the vest he was wearing. A cigarette dangled from his mouth and he reeked of sweat and beer.

"Yer to fill the fire bin," he told them.

"We're just putting our stuff down," Jo said without looking directly at him.

"While you're at it, girl, you can sweep the path," Edward Dwyer insisted. "And you ain't done the lawn, boy."

"We've got homework to do," Tom countered.

"You're late! If yer'd come home on time, yer could've done yer work by now."

"We were kept in," Jo told him coldly.

"No excuse, girl. Yer get into trouble at school, yer still gotta do your chores here. Get outside and do it, yer'll get no tea 'til yer done."

Their Uncle stood waiting for them to re-emerge from their rooms and then stood outside chain-smoking several cigarettes, making sure they worked. When dinner was ready, he glared at them – almost daring them to stop working – before going into the house and locking the door. He seemed to find their rebellious expressions amusing.

"Bastard," Tom muttered. He knew better than to call his Uncle that to his face.

"Just keep working," Jo urged. "He can't keep us out all night."

"I wouldn't put it past him!" Tom retorted quietly.

The option of coming right out and arguing with their Uncle was not even considered. They had done that once – and only once. His punishment had been harsh and painful – and they had been in the right. Their Uncle had simply not wanted to listen; he only wanted to dominate them. So now, they were careful not to provoke him.

"He wouldn't dare if Ted were here," Tom continued. "Anyway, I wonder why the lowlife isn't at work this evening."

"From his stench, he probably had to work today," Jo suggested. "We didn't allow for that."

Jo had started moving briquettes from the pile in the driveway to the shed at the back using her old child's wheelbarrow. Even though stooping made her back ache, it was still faster than carrying armfuls as Tom was doing.

The evening was coming over cold and clouds were building, making the evening seem like it was dusk already. It was dark in fact before they finished carrying all the briquettes around to the back and filled the bin by the back door.

When they tried to re-enter the house, they found that the back door, like the front, was locked. Neither had their keys on them.

After knocking for five minutes, without being let in, they sat down on the step and muttered curses they would like visited on their Uncle.

It would be is doing. Aunt Hilda wouldn't do this to them. When 'he' wasn't around, she let them do their own thing. When 'he' was at home, she never went against his decisions.

It was some time later, when they were cold, stiff, hungry and angry, they heard the door being unlocked.

They wasted no time getting inside, slipping into the kitchen and washing their hands in the sink. Their meals were on the table, covered and cold.

Halfway through the no longer appetising meal, they heard their brother arrive home. He had a key to the front door, and from the front room, they could hear their Uncle giving him a genial greeting and Aunt Hilda offering to get his dinner from the oven.

"All sweet and domestic," Tom muttered resentfully, continuing to eat, even though he would have liked to chuck the rest of his meal in the bin.

"Evening, Tom. Evening, Jo," Ted Dwyer greeted cheerfully. His sister and brother simply glared back. Neither was in a polite, sociable mood.

"Like that is it?" Ted commented, more to himself, and he went upstairs to change out of his police uniform.

He returned, five minutes later and sat down at the table. Aunt Hilda retrieved his meal from the oven.

"You finally did the lawn, then," Ted commented to Tom. "Looked good, what I could see of it."

Tom ignored him.

"Uncle mentioned that you were kept in at school today."

"Sort of," Jo said, not looking at her brother. "One of the shelves in the home room cupboard collapsed. We were helping sort out the mess, since we walk home and didn't have to race out and catch a bus."

Ted nodded, satisfied, and began to eat his tea.

After a while, the effect of utter silence from his siblings began to bother him.

His attempts at conversation were ignored until after they heard the front door slam shut, loudly.

"You want to know what's bothering me?" Tom suddenly exploded.

"It's him! Do you know what he did? He locked us out until we'd done the lawn and the paths and moved the damn briquettes."

"One way to get the job done," Ted said mildly. The lawn had been too long for several weeks. "You didn't need to back-chat him. You know you are meant to help around here."

Tom looked at the kitchen ceiling and seemed to be counting. He had his anger in check when he answered.

"All I said was that I had homework to do," Tom said. "I didn't even mention that the reason I hadn't done the lawn sooner, apart from the fact that the ground has been too wet, was because the mower was out of fuel. I asked Aunt for some money to get some, but she didn't have any."

"You could have asked me or used some of your pocket money. I would have paid it back to you," Ted said calmly.

"There is no way – I will spend my money – on mower fuel for him!" Tom said. "And you aren't usually around when the mowing subject comes up."

Tom wasn't about to mention that he had spent all his pocket money on items for their tricks.

Jo broke in, "He didn't have to keep us outside till our tea was stone cold and we'd been freezing out there for over an hour - after we'd finished."

She sounded resentful. "Now I have a really rotten headache. I'm too tired to concentrate and I wanted to finish my science assignment tonight."

"I'll let you stay up a bit," Ted offered. "And I'll get the fire going in the lounge."

"Why doesn't he get a gas heater installed?" Jo said. "It would be cheaper to run and pollute the air less. Besides, Aunt Hilda would be able to use it more easily and she wouldn't have to worry about lighting the fire. She hates that, and won't let us do it."

"Gas heaters cost money," Ted sighed. "We're lucky to be able to live here with Uncle as it is. Look, I'll talk to him. I'll see if he will consider it, and maybe I can put a bit more aside to help pay for it."

He was already paying money to Uncle for their board, as well as paying for his sibling's schooling.

"Why don't you both go and wash off the rest of the coal dust and come and work in the lounge."

"Alright," Jo agreed, deciding that she couldn't eat any more. She scraped her plate into the bin and rinsed it before going upstairs to monopolise the shower.

Tom followed her actions, but went out to the laundry to use the old concrete tub there to wash the rest of the coal dust from his face and arms.

Though Tom and Jo claimed to want to finish their assignment, it wasn't much use. They had only made the claim to support their argument about their Uncle, and only decided to make the effort to do it because their brother was being reasonable. They did like pleasing him but they were virtually asleep over their work.

Ted grinned faintly, woke them both and sent them to bed.

"Can you finish it tomorrow?" he asked.

"Yeah, no prob's," Tom yawned.

Chapter 3

Science was the first subject in the morning after homeroom. As the class was walking from there to the science lab, Tom and Jo kept their heads down, waiting for the comments when people saw the arrangement of the wheelie bins.

Instead of the neat line – waiting to be taken around the grounds, the bins were lying on the ground, in circles around the flagpoles.

"What the…" was all they heard Mr Rhodes say.

The students of Ten Silver began to chuckle.

Tom and Jo had left home early – arriving at school just as the truck finished emptying the bins. The groundsman had gratefully accepted their offer to fill in time by taking the bins to where they had to go.

Rhodes glanced at Tom and Jo, but dismissed his suspicions. They were acting no differently to the rest of the class and they had raced into the homeroom after the first bell – late again.

In fact, they seemed more subdued than normal. Either they had taken his warning seriously, or they had more mischief planned. If that was the case – nothing had better fall down in his lab.

"Did you finish your assignment?" Jo's friend, Julie Mitchell asked.

Jo shook her head. "Had to help our Aunt with stuff."

"Mum says you are welcome to come over any time to study," Julie offered, concerned for her friend. "She'll pick you up and drop you off – or you can come home on the bus with me."

"Thanks for the offer, Jules," Jo smiled. "But we'll manage."

Julie refrained from commenting further. Jo had a large collection of excuses for why she couldn't come over and used them also for explaining to teachers why her homework was late, incomplete or non-existent.

Julie shook her head and mentally shrugged. It was inexplicable to her why Jo didn't care about her work. Sometimes she and her brother worked well, and then there were times like this when they didn't care if they were reprimanded for not working. Jo gave the excuse that things were too dull and needed livening up – and someone had to do it.

Though couldn't they work and play tricks?

Julie pretended to be concentrating on the section of her science book that they had all been told to read. She had seen Rhodes start heading in her direction. She had known he would. Everyone except Tom and Jo had placed their assignments on the front bench as they came in.

"Jo, have you got your assignment?" Rhodes asked, coming up to where Jo sat next to Julie.

Jo looked up, seemed to recall that she should have had it. "Darn. I left it in the lounge room last night. I'll bring it tomorrow."

"Don't bother," Rhodes said in his mildest tone. "I'm not accepting late submissions."

He moved off to talk to Tom.

For a moment Jo frowned, recalling the previous evening, then she grinned.

"Oh well, at least I don't have to finish the darn thing."

Jo went back to reading her book.

By chance, her eyes met those of her brother; they grinned at each other. Their morning prank had buoyed their spirits.

Midway through the period, whilst Rhodes was demonstrating a series of chemical reactions, a senior student delivered him a message. He glanced at it, frowned, told the messenger that he would deal with it, and then went on with his lesson.

When his students were in turn investigating other reactions, Rhodes wrote a note and sent the nearest student to take it to the deputy principal.

What he had written was – "If it was their intention to be sent out of class to right their mess, I would rather they stayed in class. They pay little enough attention in class as it is. I'll speak to them."

In fact, Tom and Jo had become engrossed in the experiments they were set and had forgotten any thoughts of mischief.

When the bell for second period rang and they had not been summoned, Tom and Jo grinned at each other and joined their class walking back to their homeroom for English.

During English, Tom and Jo had the perfect excuse to leave class. They needed to go to the library to change their reading text for class. Armed with an official permission slip, they dawdled to the library but were unlucky enough to encounter the vice principal, Hendry.

"Why are you out of class?" he demanded, startling them as they approached the library building. Jo jumped and spun around.

"Sir, we're just going to change our set text book."

Jo managed to sound polite and Tom produced their two books and the permission slip.

Hendry nodded seeing the slip was legitimate.

"Make it quick," he cautioned, allowing them to continue.

Both Dwyers grinned as they scurried the final distance to the library.

They had managed to waste twenty minutes by the time they returned and ignored the reprimand and the injunction to get the notes they had missed from a classmate.

On their return, they had noticed that the wheelie bins were now in their correct places.

At first break, Tom went off to play ball with some of the other year ten boys. Jo stayed with Julie. They each had different elective classes from the boys until lunchtime.

"Why would you want to do what he wants?" Jo asked her brother before the afternoon classes started. "Jackson's a twit. Besides, where would he get twenty dollars? He's forever broke. And if he had that much, why give it away?"

Tom shrugged. "Who cares? I can use the cash and it is hardly the first time we have cut classes and not been missed. I like the idea of skipping maths."

Jo had to agree. The risk factor was low; the ego boost factor was high.

"Tell him that for double that, we'll both do it," Jo suggested slyly.

If Jackson had that much money to waste, they might as well oblige him.

Maths was the last period before homeroom and both Tom and Jo were heads down and working hard or at least doing enough work to convince the nearsighted Mr Nesbitt that they were.

Just about everyone in the room knew what the Dwyers were planning and thought it a great joke. And since the perpetrators did not seem concerned about being caught and everyone agreed that Jackson needed to be outwitted, the class were prepared to cover their absence. Jo's friend Julie and Tom's friend Mike had agreed to collect their friends' belongings.

The window was already open and Tom was simply waiting for the right opportunity.

When a message came for Nesbitt about a phone call, Tom acted quickly and Jo moved to where Tom had been sitting.

Nesbitt instructed the class to keep working quietly, seemed satisfied that they would, and left the room.

Moments later, Jo was out the window and dashing past the canteen and around it to the maintenance shed. They were to meet Fred Jackson there.

"Where is he?" Jo asked with eyebrows raised suggestively.

Tom grinned maliciously. "Maybe he got caught sneaking out?"

"I doubt it. Ten Green have sport this session," Jo reminded him.

"Right, all he'd have to do is give Mr. T. cheek and he'd have to do ten laps of the school," Tom agreed.

The prediction was correct. Moments later, Fred Jackson approached the maintenance shed, seemed to stop to catch his breath and wait for his mate Tim Tyson to catch up.

Tom emerged from the shed.

"Cough up, Jackson," he demanded.

"All right! Keep your shirt on – you win." Jackson agreed with a hint of ill humour. "I'll meet you at the front gate after school."

"Don't dawdle then. We're getting picked up today."

Jo thought that Jackson looked startled, but he hid it by beginning to run on the spot.

"If you get found out before then, the deal's off."

"No it's not. The deal was to get out of maths without Nesbitt seeing us go."

"S'right Jacko," Tyson agreed, having caught up and heard the remarks. Jackson snarled at Tyson, then suddenly grinned

"Yeah, right. After school then."

Jackson seemed quite agreeable now. He and Tyson jogged off.

"Well, what now?" Jo asked, watching out the window. "Do we hang around for homeroom or what?"

"If Ted wasn't picking us up – I'd go home," Tom admitted. "How long before the bell?"

"Half an hour," Jo advised.

"We might as well wait here. The maintenance guys are finished for the day. Just before the bell we can head back via the library."

It was unfortunate that some of the groundsmen hadn't finished and needed to get tools from the maintenance shed. They noticed it was unlocked and went in.

"What are you students doing here?" the older man asked sternly. "How'd you get in?"

"Nothing," Jo assured them quickly, jumping up from the box she was sitting on.

Tom stayed perched on a second box. "The door was unlocked and we decided to come in here and talk. We have a free period and we can't talk in the library."

"You should know you aren't allowed in here," the man insisted.

"We haven't touched anything," Jo assured him. "We only came in when we realised it wasn't locked."

She smiled at the man and his stern gaze relented.

"What's your name and class?" he asked more kindly. "I'll keep quiet this time – but if you come in again – I'll have to mention it."

Tom nodded at Jo.

"Jo Dwyer," she admitted. "Ten Silver."

"Tom Dwyer, ditto."

"You're twins, aren't you?"

"No, Tom's older," Jo admitted. "I usually tell people that I skipped a grade because of my academic brilliance." Jo grinned at the gardeners.

"When in fact, I was ill when I was due to start school, so I was kept back a year," Tom grinned. "Actually, I'm older by ten months."

Both gardeners grinned at the joke. The older man told Tom and Jo to "Nick off," which they did with alacrity, managing to blend in with a group of year nine students who were taking measurements outside.

Fred Jackson had seen the gardeners enter the shed and the Dwyers leave, and deliberately stopped again outside the shed and gave a shrill whistle. The gardeners did not emerge.

"Psst, Tom," Jackson called loud enough to be heard inside.

"What do you want?" was the reply as one of the gardeners emerged. Jackson pretended to be taken by surprise.

"Ah, nothing!"

"Can't be nothing. You expected your little mate to be here, didn't you?"

Jackson didn't answer immediately. When he did, anyone who knew him slightly would have wondered at his uncharacteristic candour. Those that knew him well would know he was causing trouble.

"Yeah, I saw Tom and Jo head in here," he admitted. "I wanted to warn them that you guys were still working and they'd better not stay in here. I also wanted to know why the heck they were climbing out of the tuckshop window. Well, I tried."

Fred Jackson jogged off slowly. Tyson was again a short distance behind, but though he slowed, he didn't stop. However, he overheard some of the ensuing conversation.

"I told you it was the canteen window!" the younger man was saying. "We'll have to report them."

Tyson jogged on and reported to Jackson who had stopped just out of sight of the shed. The two were smirking as they completed the final lap of the school.

"He never noticed," Julie told Jo. "We were all working when he came back – so he just kept on with the lesson."

The two girls had just got to the homeroom.

"Good," Jo commented with satisfaction, and took her books from her friend.

"Why do you do it?" Julie asked Jo with exasperation.

"It's fun," Jo grinned. "Besides, I'm sick of having to get a pass to go anywhere during lesson time - particularly for urgent calls of nature."

Julie groaned. "That I agree with. But aren't you worried about being in trouble?"

"They don't do anything – just chew you out!" Jo shrugged. "Words won't hurt you."

Just as everyone was sitting down in their seats, the PA system was activated.

"Message for all staff. There will be a short, special staff meeting, directly after final bell. Everyone must attend. The following students are asked to come to student foyer…"

A list of names followed.

"…And all students who were involved in outside activities during last period should also come to student foyer."

Mike whispered to Tom, "Are you going?"

"No way," Tom said fervently. "If they figure out we were out of class, we lose that bet with Jackson. At least we have heaps of witnesses to say Nesbitt never noticed."

Rhodes continued with his afternoon messages.

At final bell, there was a great deal of speculation as to what was going on, and why so many students were summoned up to the admin building. Nobody had a clue, so the topic soon died. Word would get around – it usually did.

Tom waited with his sister at the front car park gate. He was eyeing off a white falcon that had the subtle signs of being a police car. A few spaces further along was Ted's car, but he wasn't in it.

"Do you think he got called in to talk about us?" Jo suggested.

"Na!" Tom disagreed. "They usually send home a letter first."

"Well, he's coming back from over there."

Tom watched his brother. "He doesn't look annoyed."

He switched his gaze to scan the thinning crowd for Fred Jackson.

"Jo! Tom!" Ted Dwyer called, waving at them.

They both picked up their bags and wondered over.

"Do you mind hanging around a while?" Ted asked them. "Someone robbed your canteen. Inspector Kent is here, investigating. He asked me to give him a hand. You can wait near the front office if you want."

"We'll wait out here," Tom said quickly. "I heard how many people were asked to go up there. Besides, I'm supposed to be getting some notes from Fred Jackson. He said he'd give them to me here, after school."

"We'll come in when he's been past," Jo promised.

Ted accepted the answer and headed back towards the administration building.

"About time!" Tom growled at Jackson.

"I thought your brother was picking you up!" Jackson commented.

"You hoped we'd be gone, you mean," Jo accused. "He's inside with Inspector Kent, helping to investigate the canteen break-in."

Jackson's expression became cautious. "He's a cop?"

Jo merely nodded. "So what did they want everyone for?"

"Just asking us if we saw anything odd," Jackson said with a dismissive shrug. "Don't worry, I didn't mention you two to them." He jerked a thumb in the direction of the Admin.

"Cough up, Fred!" Tom reminded Jackson. "I can see Ted coming back."

Jackson didn't look, but drew two new looking but rumpled twenty-dollar notes from his pocket. He squashed them into Tom's hand and walked off quickly. Tom pocketed them at once.

"Do you think he's got a guilty conscience?" Tom smirked.

"Probably," Jo agreed, knowing that Tom had lied about Ted approaching. "If half of what he claims about his old man is true – I'd stay clear of the police too, in case they thought I was as bad."

"It wouldn't mean he was," Tom allowed, "But then again, he says his old man is mates with our Uncle – that's hardly a recommendation either."

"When did he tell you that?"

"A week or so ago. Before Uncle came back this time. I was going to mention it, but it slipped my mind until just now."

"Makes me wonder what He really does when he's away," Jo said snidely.

"Ted would never let us stay with him, if he thought Uncle was a crook," Tom protested.

"Well, I'd believe that of him," Jo accused. She knew that Tom probably felt the same way, even if he did seem to be giving the creep the benefit of the doubt.

"You know he's got Ted convinced that he's a jolly old dock walloper who can't help the roughnecks he has to work with."

"Yeah, and that we are unruly beasts," Tom finally agreed. "Should we go in?"

"I'd rather wait out here," Jo decided. It was probably better not to be seen with their brother if the subject of their pranks came into any teacher's mind.

The buses had all finally left, the stream of students leaving from the admin building had ceased and most of the teachers had left before they saw Ted and his superior walking towards them.

Inspector Kent greeted them with a smile.

"Sorry for hijacking your chauffer and making you wait," he said. "As it was I hadn't come here on business in the first place."

Tom and Jo grinned back. They knew Inspector Kent quite well, from police social occasions, and were friends with his children, twins – William and Wendy.

"I've moved into my mother's place," Kent went on. "It's only a few streets from your place. I'll be doing it up in my spare time. I came to arrange for Will and Wendy to come to school here."

"Are we allowed to ask what's going on?" Jo asked, avidly curious. "Fred said the canteen was broken into."

"Yes, it seems that it was. Though only the five and ten dollar notes were missing," Kent told them.

"But…" Tom prompted, sensing something more to the story.

"But, it's more complicated than that," Ted finished.

Both Tom and Jo knew they would not be told anything else.

"Anything we can do?" Jo asked instead.

"Just keep your eyes open," Kent suggested thoughtfully. "Let your brother know if anyone seems to have more money than usual."

Kent had glanced away, so he did not see the uncomfortable flush on Jo's face. A vision of Fred Jackson had come into her mind – but she did not dare mention him.

"I'll see you in the morning, Dwyer," Kent dismissed his subordinate.

Ted nodded in reply and followed his siblings to his car. He was pleased to see that they were in a better mood.

Chapter 4

The following morning, their pleasant mood quickly evaporated when their Uncle contrived to delay their departure for school. They had deliberately left for school early, intending to be gone before he got home. However, they had only gone the distance of a few houses when their Uncle had passed them, stopped and ordered them back home to help him move some boxes.

As a result, they arrived late for homeroom, only to discover that their homeroom was empty. The adjoining rooms were likewise deserted, so they realised that a special assembly must have been called. They hurried to the hall.

Late arrivals had to sit at the back and had their names recorded. They were told to report to the student foyer after assembly.

All they heard of the assembly was the Vice Principal asking all students to watch out for any strangers hanging around the school and report any such to their homeroom teachers.

Four other students had arrived late; two had notes, one claimed he was delayed by the late arrival of his bus and the other was limping so badly that his reason for being late was obvious. That one went directly to the school nurse.

Mr Hendry finally turned to the Dwyers.

"Sixth time in three weeks," he remarked. His voice held no note of leniency.

"What was it this time?"

"We were moving boxes of stuff for our Aunt. She wants to start painting the spare room today," Jo said sourly. That was the reason their Uncle had given them.

"Then why didn't you get her to write you a note?" he asked them reasonably.

It was no use telling him that their Uncle flatly refused to do it and Aunt Hilda had gone to the shops.

"We thought we could still get here in time if we ran all the way,"

Tom said instead. "We didn't allow for having to hunt for everyone, Sir."

"Perhaps," Hendry allowed. "Come into my office."

Hendry turned and expected to be followed. Jo glanced at Tom with alarm. This wasn't normal practice. If they were going to get detention, he would have said so, then sent them back to their class.

Hendry sat behind his desk, but didn't offer his 'guests' a seat.

"Why were you both in the maintenance shed yesterday?"

Hendry saw the shock of his question on the faces of both students.

"Who told you we were?" Jo asked cautiously.

"Were you?"

After a moment, Tom nodded.

"Why?"

"We skipped out of Maths, Sir," Tom finally admitted. He looked at Hendry's desk, not the Vice-Principal's face.

"Why?"

Tom was tempted to mention Fred Jackson, but didn't want to snitch.

When they didn't answer, Hendy asked another question.

"How did you get in? I was told that the maintenance manager had already locked the shed."

"It wasn't locked," Jo told him truthfully.

"And did you find it inexplicably open again this morning too?" Hendry asked, intently.

"We were nowhere near it this morning," Tom argued, looking up. "We told you where we were."

"When did you leave yesterday? You were seen at the gate well after the bell."

"We left after you had finished with Inspector Kent and our brother. Ted drove us home," Jo told him.

A look of enlightenment showed on Hendry's face.

"You are related to Constable Dwyer," he clarified.

"Yes, Sir," Tom admitted.

"How did you get red paint on your hands, Jo?" Hendry asked suddenly.

Jo glanced at her hands.

"Uncle had red paint on him when he got home," Jo recalled aloud. "I must have got it on me when I took a box from him. I really hadn't noticed."

Jo tried to wipe the paint from her hands onto her dress.

"Hmm," Hendry vocalised. He didn't feel that the students were lying to him, but he had to find out certain other facts.

"The maintenance shed was sprayed with red paint, sometime last night," Hendry watched for a reaction.

"We never…" Tom exploded. Hendry silenced him with a look.

"What about the bins yesterday morning?"

"That was just a bit of fun!" Jo protested.

"And the projector screen and the cupboard and the picture?"

"A joke!" Tom insisted.

"Mrs Burgess didn't think the joke was funny."

"I found the photo on the school website," Jo admitted. "I didn't know it as her. I thought she'd see it as funny too." But not at first, she silently amended.

"So do you expect me to believe that you two wouldn't consider some painting – as just a bit of fun?" Hendry challenged them.

"We didn't do it!" Tom insisted again.

Hendry stared at them thoughtfully.

"Turn out your bags!"

"What?" Tom looked startled.

Hendry did not repeat himself. He simply waited for them to obey.

Jo gave in first and squatted down to remove folders and books from her backpack. She placed everything in a neat pile on the floor. Then to prove it was empty, she tipped her bag upside down and shook it. She lost all colour in her face when she saw the ultra-wide red texta fall from her pack.

"Thomas," Hendry prompted.

Tom felt himself become shaky. He pulled his books out with equal care, trying at the same time to fell for anything that shouldn't be there. His fingers touched what he thought at first was an empty drink can, except it was sticky on the outside.

He stretched out the task, trying to give himself time to think. Who could have put the can of paint in there? Even without producing it, he was sure that is what it would be. When could it have been put there? It had to have been recent, even if he hadn't emptied his bag in ages. An answer eluded him.

There was nothing else for it. If he tried to hide it – he'd look guilty. Heck, it looked that way anyway. Tom placed the spray can beside his books and shook his backpack as his sister had done.

Hendy looked to be disappointed, as if he had caught them lying to him.

"Bring that can and the pen over here," he directed.

He noticed that both students held the items by an edge, as if they were evidence. That was interesting.

"Do you both still claim innocence?"

"Yes!" both Tom and Jo said at once.

"Well then," Hendry began slowly, watching both students as he spoke. "Why were you both seen climbing out of the canteen window yesterday?"

"No!" Tom argued. He quickly realised how things looked. "We did not climb out of the canteen window."

Damn, they were in strife already…what the heck?

"I told you we skipped out of Maths," Tom stared helplessly at his sister. Jo nodded her agreement. "Well, we climbed out of the maths room window; it's next to the canteen window."

"More fun?" Hendry prompted.

"It was at the time," Tom said in a small voice.

"And your teacher didn't notice?" Hendry sounded sceptical.

"Mr. Nesbitt was out of the room for a moment," Tom told him. It wasn't his intention to get the teacher into trouble.

"Our friends knew we'd been put up to it and covered for us," Jo added in explanation. "I don't want them in trouble – they did try to talk us out of it."

"When was this?"

"Half past two, about," Tom calculated. "Might have been a bit before."

Hendry nodded – unfortunately, the timing was about right.

"So who put you up to it?" Hendry asked finally.

Tom said disgustedly, "Does it matter, Sir? We're the idiots that agreed to it and did it."

"It might matter," Hendry counselled them. "The police might want to know – there is more to the canteen theft than just robbery."

"Ted said that much," Jo said quietly. "But he didn't say what it was."

Hendry was glad it wasn't up to him to decide the guilt or innocence of these two students. That was a police matter and he would be advising them of what he'd learnt.

As for the breaches of school rules, it was time these two students stopped thinking they could get away with unacceptable behaviour.

"I'll be drafting a letter for you to take home at the end of the day," he told the students. "There will be a section that needs to be returned by your parents, or rather your Uncle. You live with him, I believe."

"He's away more often than not!" Jo said. "Anyway, he's not our guardian, Ted is."

Hendry did not disagree with them; he would check their file.

"In the meantime, both of you can help clean off the paint in the maintenance shed."

"We didn't do that!" Tom argued, forgetting courtesy and getting angry.

"You will help clean up the mess, young man, or a week of lunchtime detention will become a week's suspension."

Tom dropped his eyes and capitulated.

"Yes, Sir."

Jo's voice echoed his reluctant agreement.

"Put your books and bags in your locker and come back here."

"Why should we clean up someone else's mess?" Tom ranted to his sister, as soon as they were out of the administration block.

"Because they need someone to do it and we're the nearest miscreants," Jo decided. "Besides, it beats English and writing essays."

Tom managed a slight grin.

"Yeah, there's that! I'll kill Fred Jackson. He set us up."

"Get real, Tom. We didn't have to agree to his silly dare," Jo reminded him. "And he would have had to have known in advance that the canteen was going to be robbed."

"He'd have known if he was going to do it," Tom argued. "Mr. T had him doing laps, and he wasn't being watched. Oh, God! I hope Hendry isn't going to write to Uncle…"

Jo silently shared that sentiment.

There was a worse shock in store for Jo when she examined the red graffiti. There was no message or picture – just sprayed paint and texta scrawls everywhere. It looked to have been done in a hurry. The shock came when she saw the two little smiley faces in a corner. It was the 'signature' she put on all the pictures she drew in art class. It was not a secret, as she made a point of it, but it meant that whoever did it, wanted her blamed - or her and Tom.

She made no comment, just used the rags and solvent on that part first.

They were allowed to stop during lunch break, but had to stay in their homeroom under the watchful eye of their homeroom teacher. Tom looked up from an assignment he was working on and saw Fred Jackson staring at them through the window. He smirked and moved off once he was seen.

At the end of the break, the rest of Ten Silver entered the room. Some subtle sense of trouble caused almost everyone to leave Tom and Jo Dwyer alone at the front of the row of tables. Julie saw the space next to Jo and took it. She felt for Jo's hand under the table and squeezed it. Jo didn't glance around, just gently squeezed back.

When everyone was settled, it became obvious that Rhodes was staying and the room became quiet. They should have been having History.

"It has come to my notice," Rhodes began, and he had the attention of the whole class, "That everyone in this class that does general maths – knew of and connived with an intentional breach of rules. What was at the time, merely a prank, has become much more serious. The culprits have owned up to their prank and have no wish for the rest of you to be punished for your part. However, certain points need clarification. I want each of you who know anything about the matter to write down what you know on a sheet of paper. You don't have to sign it if you choose not to."

Rhodes handed everyone a sheet of paper.

"When you finish, fold the paper in quarters and leave it on my desk."

When Rhodes wasn't looking, Mike met Tom's gaze. Tom just shrugged. Mike took it to mean he should do what he felt was right.

Rhodes made no comment as students wandered up and placed folded papers on the desk. When all that intended to write anything had, he told the class to find some work to finish and put all the notes in his folder.

Rhodes paused by Tom on his way out at the end of the lesson.

"Call by the office on your way out, for a letter."

Tom nodded.

As soon as he was out of the room, Mike and several other students formed a group around Tom and Jo.

"How much trouble are you in?" Mike demanded of his friend.

"More than we asked for," Tom sighed, his eyes flicking around the circle. He wondered if his classmates would help him.

"Someone vandalised the maintenance shed last night, with red texta and paint," Tom told them. "This time it wasn't us, but whoever it was put the texta and paint can in our bags. We spent the morning cleaning up their mess."

"I'll ask around and see if anyone has been hanging around our lockers," Mike promised. "When might it have been?"

"That's just it! The damage was done last night after we left or before we got here this morning. We got here late for the assembly. The only time we didn't have our bags was during the last few minutes of the assembly – we left them outside. We went straight to the admin after that."

Mike nodded. "I'll still ask around," he promised.

The group had to break up when their language teacher arrived.

Chapter 5

After the final bell, Tom and Jo went to the student foyer to pick up the letter they had to take home. The receptionist knew nothing about it and went to ask for it. Vice Principal Hendry returned with her and following them was Edward Dwyer.

Tom's initial reaction was one of amazement. His Uncle was dressed in a suit and looked eminently respectable; nothing like his normal self. His second reaction was the gut blow of seeing him there at school.

"What's he doing here?" Jo whispered. "I bet Hendry called him."

"Tom. Jo," Edward Dwyer greeted his niece and nephew, acting like a concerned parent.

"The school called me. Told me about the trouble you are in. I can't say I approve of your behaviour. I have been advised that you are not to be suspended, but the school will not tolerate any more misbehaviour. What do you have to say for yourselves?"

Neither Tom nor Jo said anything, they just glared back at their uncle. They saw a flash of amusement on his face and began feeling sick.

Edward Dwyer gave Hendry a 'See what I mean?' look.

"Come on, I'll drive you home."

They had no choice but to follow him and made no effort to hide their reluctance.

Dwyer said nothing to them all the way home. Tom and Jo, sharing the back seat of his Commodore, exchanged only glances. It was unnerving – watching their Uncle pretending to be the opposite of what he really was and waiting fearfully for him to revert to normal.

The dreaded transformation occurred after they had walked through the front door. Dwyer removed his jacket and loosened his tie, then fixed his nephew and niece in place with a look.

"You are both grounded for two weeks," he pronounced with a smirk. "You will not leave for school until I've got home and you will be home before I leave."

"What if you're late home?" Tom asked, keeping his voice neutral.

"Then you can stay home and work around here or walk faster to school. If I find out that you wagged school, I'll thrash you."

Dwyer was satisfied with their reactions. They were obviously scared of him.

"I was telling your Vice principal some home truths about you. He'll be wise to your ways from now on."

"What have you been saying?" Jo blurted imprudently.

A very swift hand reached across to her and slapped her face hard.

"What needed saying," Dwyer snarled. "Both of you go to your rooms and stay there, except for meals."

Jo controlled herself until she reached her room. Once inside, she locked the door and threw her pack across the floor. Moments later she was crying into her pillow.

After a while, she became aware of her brother calling her name, softly.

Wiping her face, Jo rolled off the bed and walked to the far corner of the room. Here there was a piece of pipe sticking from the wall. It was the diameter of a ten-cent piece. She reached into her drawer and pulled out an empty can with a similar sized hole in the base. When this was fitted on the end of the pipe, it completed a crude but efficient intercom. She could talk to her brother.

"Do you think he'll tell Ted?" Jo asked after assuring Tom she was all right.

"Sure to, just to gloat," Tom told her. "Couldn't you see it? He's enjoying us being in trouble."

"Could he have vandalised the shed at school? He had red paint on him this morning," Jo asked Tom's opinion.

"Coincidence, Sis. Why would he? You know what a lazy swine he is."

The conversation flagged after a while and they agreed to disable the intercom. Jo put her tin away and replaced her heavy winter coat on the pipe 'hook'.

She wondered if they would get tea that night and dreaded what Ted would say.

Jo was dozing when the front door slamming awakened her. She heard Ted clearly.

"Where are they?"

She had never heard Ted use that tone before and for the first time in her life dreaded seeing him.

"Tom! Jo! Get down here!" Ted yelled. "Now!'

Jo groaned; she knew she had better do as he said. Tom met her at the door and they exchanged glances.

Ted watched his brother and sister as they came down the stairs. From the corner of his eye, he could see his uncle loitering in the hall; listening without doubt.

With a gesture of his hand, he indicated that he wanted to talk in the lounge room. He followed his siblings and closed both doors.

"Sit!" he instructed, and he watched both Tom and Jo perch on the edge of the couch.

"Do either of you realise the perfectly horrible position you have put me in?" Ted said in a loud voice. "No? Kent is going to question you. That is bad enough, but what is worse is that my superiors are questioning my honesty and integrity. I have been told that I might have to step down – until the mess you are in is sorted out!"

"We're sorry…" Jo tried to say.

"Sorry! It's too late for sorry!" Ted continued to speak loudly, but all the time he had been looking at the door to the hall, not his siblings.

"Go upstairs and grab a coat! We're going out."

"Out where?" Tom asked, subdued.

"Never mind, damn where," Ted retorted. "Somewhere where I can tell you what I think of you without having to modify it for polite company."

Tom and Jo slunk upstairs.

Ted went and found his uncle, who had moved away from listening at the door.

"Thanks for going to the school, Uncle. I am sorry you were put out. You should have called me. They're my responsibility, not yours."

"Just trying to help, my boy," Dwyer said in the genial tone he used with his oldest nephew. "Where are you off to?"

"Down to the station at Footscray," Ted claimed in a lower voice. "Kent wants to question them. We may not be back until late."

"I told you that you are too soft on them, boy!" Dwyer claimed. "They need a good hiding."

Ted ignored the advice as he herded his siblings outside and into the police car that he had waiting at the gate. He opened the back door for them.

"Where are we going?" Tom asked suspiciously.

Ted waited until he was in the driver's seat to answer.

"Not the station, though Uncle thinks we are," Ted said in a much modified tone. "Buckle up!"

Ted started the car and moved off from the kerb.

"I'm sorry for the carry on back there, but I had my reasons for letting Uncle think I was mad at you."

"So, are you really mad at us?" Jo asked in a quiet voice.

"Some, you idiots. Now, I don't intend to say any more until we get where we are going. It isn't far."

Ted drove for less than five minutes before pulling up outside an old terrace house. He got out and went around to open the door for Tom and Jo to get out.

"Funny police station," Tom managed to jest.

Ted just grinned and walked to the front door. He rang the bell and waited.

Jo and Tom felt instantly better the moment they recognised Will Kent in the opened door way.

"Come in," Will invited. "Dad's waiting. Go on through to the room right at the back."

Jo felt herself relax. Whatever was planned – it wasn't official. She was able to grin at Wendy Kent when they reached the rearmost room.

Inspector Kent shooed his daughter out and invited his guests to sit. He offered refreshments, which confused Tom and Jo, as they didn't know what to expect.

Ted sat back and let his superior handle the coming interview.

"I told Constable Dwyer to bring you here because I want to talk to you; unofficially at the moment. I may yet decide to make it official –

not because I think you are guilty of a criminal offence, but because it might be necessary to provide cause for further investigation. I will be recording the interview. Will you both co-operate?"

He received two nods.

"Good, because your brother has put his reputation on the line for you and I am taking the responsibility for telling you some highly classified information."

Two pairs of eyes watched Kent, intently.

"Your Mr. Hendry called me this morning after his interview with you. He appreciated that you did not want to name the person who put you up to your dare of leaving class, but I was not so impressed. I suggested that your classmates be asked about the incident in such a way that no one could be directly accused of dobbing. You have some very loyal friends who had fewer scruples about laying blame."

"So you know who put us up to our little stunt, do you?" Jo asked.

"The Jackson boy – and he was going to pay twenty dollars to each of you if you succeeded in remaining unchallenged for the rest of the day. Is that how it was?"

Tom nodded.

"Do you still have the money he gave you?"

Tom pulled out his wallet and extracted the money. Kent took it carefully by the edges and carried it over to a lamp. He smiled, grimly.

"I'll just keep these," Kent told Tom. "They are truly artistic forgeries."

Tom looked up, startled. "How did Fred get forgeries?"

"We'd like to know that too," Kent admitted. "Jackson made a mistake giving these to you. Though, it was probably another subtle ploy to get you in trouble."

"Like putting my art signature on the vandalised shed," Jo added sourly. She had not even mentioned that to Tom.

"Probably," Kent agreed. "Now, the canteen break-in. It looked as if the thief was interrupted before he could take more than the five and ten dollar notes. That was before the canteen manager took the rest of the money to the bank. A keen eyed teller noted identical serial numbers on several twenty-dollar notes. So we come to the question of why the Jackson boy was trying to implicate the two of you. He was the one who convinced the gardeners that you had come out of the canteen window and they were the ones who told the principal."

"I told you he set us up," Tom growled at Jo.

"Details aside, why would Jackson want to get you in trouble?"

"For fun!" Tom suggested. "Because we are idiots."

"I won't argue with that!" Ted muttered. "You gave him the perfect basis to blame you."

"Give the matter some thought," Kent urged. "It may be that you can give us a clue to breaking a major forgery racket."

Kent turned off his recorder and withdrew from the room for a moment.

Jo spoke into the silence. "Fred told Tom that his dad and Uncle are mates."

Ted looked startled, he thought for a moment.

"It may be coincidence. Uncle works at the docks. There are lots of men there who wouldn't want us prying into their business."

"Fred makes a lot of claims about his old man," Tom explained, "But I've never heard it said that he works at the docks."

"It might pay for us to find out more about Fred Jackson's father," Ted thought aloud.

"Do you think Fred will get into trouble about egging us on," Tom asked his brother.

"That's a school matter," Ted shrugged. "Will Jackson come back at you if he does?"

"I can handle him," Tom proclaimed, mentally crossing his fingers. "We can avoid him at recess and we've got detention for the next four lunchtimes…"

Ted sighed. "That's another matter. Will you please promise me that you will behave at school? I don't need to get phone calls about you misbehaving. And you are on very precarious grounds at the moment. Do you want to get expelled?"

"No," Tom and Jo spoke together.

"Then why, why, why do you keep playing up at school?"

"Because we want to," Jo told him bluntly. "We know how far we can go and we don't care if we have detention. It means that we can at least get more of our assignments done."

"And by the time we get home, if we're kept in, Uncle has usually left for work," Tom said. "And he can't give us jobs that we have to finish before tea. And if he's amused by us being in trouble he's not as obnoxious."

"Why can't you do your schoolwork after tea?" Ted asked reasonably, ignoring the comments about their Uncle.

"I can't work in my room, the light is lousy," Jo complained. "I tried putting a brighter globe in. Not only did he tear strips off me for doing it – the damn thing blew the next night anyway. I tried again several times when he wasn't around and the same thing happened each time. Put anything brighter than 25W in it and it blows."

"Did you ask him about it?"

"Yes."

"And?"

"The lousy skinflint told me he couldn't afford to do anything about it. The wiring in the house is old."

"I won't tolerate you calling Uncle names," Ted told Jo sternly. "He's doing what he can. It's good of him to let us stay with him, and support us."

"Bull…," Tom retorted. "You are paying him to let us stay there. You pay for what we eat, the power, the water, our schooling – aren't you?"

"Yes, well," Ted agreed. "It's only right."

"So what's it costing him?" Jo added.

"Why do you both insist on running him down?" Ted exploded. "You are always arguing with him. He complains about you all the time."

Tom stood up and walked to face his brother.

"We – do – not – argue – with – him! Once, and only that once, we stood up for ourselves. That was enough. We took your advice – we go along with him, we do his lousy chores, only because you asked us to. But he won't accept 'we'll do it after we finish our homework' or 'in a sec, we just have to change'. If we don't do as he says he'll thrash us and enjoy doing it."

"Does he say that?" Ted asked.

"He has occasionally," Jo added. "I have no doubts that he would."

"I really think you are exaggerating," Ted told them. "He really worries about you two."

Tom snorted. "He's really got you convinced he's a genial fellow, but he's not. He's all sweet with you!"

"He treats Aunt Hilda well enough."

"That's Aunt Hilda, not us. But again, that's only when you are around," Jo insisted. "The rest of the time he is continually telling her that she is as brainless as a canary – and she believes it. He has her convinced that she is only smart enough to drudge around the house, potter about the garden and knit jumpers for him. She is convinced that if she tried to light the fire – that she would burn the house down. So when he isn't around wanting it lit she won't and she won't let us either."

"Aunt Hilda isn't the brightest of women," Ted explained patiently.

"Nah!" Jo argued. "She's been conditioned to be stupid. When he's not around to tell her what she knows or doesn't, can or can't do, and I touch on a subject he hasn't brainwashed her on – she is very smart. She can remember recipes she read once in a magazine – years ago. She can recite poems she learnt at school – and did you know that she has a Bachelor of Business Management?"

It was obvious Ted didn't.

"I saw it once. Melbourne Uni, 1956," Jo admitted triumphantly.

"Where did you see that?" Ted demanded.

"I… forget where now," Jo said hurriedly.

"Were you poking around where you shouldn't have been?" Ted eyed her sternly.

Jo eyed him back and didn't answer.

"I warned you about poking around," Ted reminded her.

"Do as you are told. Don't rock the boat," Jo mimicked that warning. "Well, yes I was. And he didn't catch me!"

"And what would he have done if he had?"

Jo's shudder was answer enough.

Ted slumped back. He knew his siblings well enough to be sure they were telling the truth.

"Have you been trying to tell me all this?" Ted asked finally.

"Yeah, but you don't listen," Tom said without anger.

"Uncle has you brainwashed too," Jo added sourly.

"Why hasn't he brainwashed you?"

"Because we are teenagers," Jo said sweetly. "It's our job to question everything our elders say and do."

As if on cue, Inspector Kent returned and spent the next half hour quizzing Tom and Jo. He asked about the routine of their school and what they knew about the activities of the canteen staff. They were surprised at exactly how much they remembered when deftly questioned by the Inspector.

Finally, "That's enough for tonight, since you both have school tomorrow. You will be seeing Will and Wendy there too. They will be starting. Could I ask you to help them settle in and try to keep them out of mischief?"

Tom's sour look changed when he realised that the Inspector was teasing them.

"We'll introduce them around," Jo promised. "What class will they be in?"

"Um, Ten Silver, I think," Kent pretended to be unsure. He had requested, in spite of sceptical looks, that they be put in with the Dwyers as his children knew them already. Now he was glad he had. Will and Wendy could help keep an eye on Tom and Jo; perhaps not keep them out of trouble, but you never knew. They could at least watch out for potential trouble.

"Whoopee," Jo cheered in delight, forgetting everything else.

"If you like Dwyer, I'll have my wife call around and pick your siblings up for school and drop them back in the afternoon."

Ted looked at his sibs and agreed.

"What if we get detention?" Tom muttered, not displeased at the suggestion of a ride to and from school.

"See that you don't," Ted countered.

"One thing I don't get," Tom commented, just after Ted began to drive them home. "How come Uncle came to the school?"

"The girl in the school office rang home asking for me. Aunt Hilda thought she meant Uncle and only took in 'trouble' and thought you had both been hurt. She called me, because there is no way she can contact Uncle at work. I told her and the school that I would come as soon as I was free. In the meantime Uncle got home, Aunt told him about the call and Uncle went to the school."

"After getting all dressed up in his best suit," Jo added.

"Apparently," Ted agreed. "Anyway, I got there after you'd left and spoke to Hendry, heard all about the trouble and how Uncle came to help the young lad, who did his best but couldn't discipline you strongly enough – and he would see to it that you didn't sneak out at night to do more mischief."

"Bet it was more than that!" Jo said, remembering her slapped face.

"A great deal more than that," Ted agreed without elaborating. "I set him straight. So what did Uncle say to you?"

"Not much," Tom shrugged. He mentioned the terms of the two-week grounding and he grinned when mentioning the part about not leaving for school until their uncle got home. "I could just see him being slow getting home so we'd be in trouble for being late," Tom explained.

A sudden thought occurred to Ted, though there seemed no logic to it. He wondered why his uncle wanted his sibs where he could find them. Was it just to keep them out of trouble?

"You said that uncle likes the idea of you being in trouble…"

"Yeah," Jo agreed.

"Well if it would make him more pleasant…"

"More condescending, more snide," Jo interrupted.

Ted ignored her comment.

"When you get home, I'll continue to act like I'm angry with you. I give you permission to stomp upstairs, slam doors and be as close to rude as I usually let you get."

"So he thinks we really are in trouble?" Jo snickered.

Tom laughed too. "How long should we keep it up?"

"Mainly for tonight," Ted decided. "Then for a few days at a mild level. A less than warm greeting when I get home, talk to me only if I talk to you first – that sort of thing."

Ted glanced in his review mirror just as he passed under a streetlight. His siblings were grinning widely. He shook his head. It was comforting to realise that whilst their uncle was apparently trying to suppress them – it wasn't working.

Ted Dwyer lay awake for a long time. He was considering many things. The most important thing was the new side to his uncle that he had learnt about that night. His instinct for trouble was nagging his mind and although he tried to ignore it – he had to consider Tom and Jo's welfare.

He was fairly sure that his uncle wasn't abusing his siblings – at least not physically. They had only ever mentioned that one incident when he had beaten them. But there were other types of abuse, including trying to destroy their credibility. Then there was that little matter of Uncle being mates with Stan Jackson. Kent had mentioned quietly that the man had a record of petty crime convictions. And what about the coincidence of the red paint, Jo and Hendry had mentioned? It had to be coincidence. Why would their uncle stoop to petty vandalism? How could he have expected to get Tom and Jo blamed? Did he even know about her art signature? It was far-fetched indeed.

But Fred Jackson had known they'd been in the shed earlier. He had incited their prank and arranged to meet there. But why? It made no sense.

Well, one thing was sure. He needed to arrange some protection for them; somewhere they could go if they felt threatened here. It seemed that Edward Dwyer behaved better when he was around, but what if he wasn't? What if something happened to him?

Ted shuddered, recalling, still vividly, the moment when his partner, Jon Daniels had died in his arms after being shot by a fleeing bandit.

He forced the memory away. But…Kath Daniels!

Yes, Ted thought, she would be perfect. Jon's mother knew Tom and Jo, she lived reasonably close by and he was sure she would look out for them if need be. It might never be necessary. He hoped it would not. He would call her tomorrow and tell Tom and Jo later.

Chapter 6

Ted told his Aunt that Gayle Kent, his superior's wife would be taking Tom and Jo to and from school. He stressed that it was to keep them out of mischief. His uncle could not argue with that!

The previous night, as his sibs had stomped upstairs, Edward Dwyer had not quite wiped off the gloating expression from his face.

His questions, meant to sound concerned, were clearly based on a hope that Tom and Jo were to be charged with something.

"What happened, Son? Anything I can do to help?"

Ted had shrugged and said, "Kent asked a lot of questions."

"Do we need to find legal advice? I know someone who could help."

"Thanks, Uncle, but there is no need. There's not enough proof to even consider laying charges."

Ted had chosen to walk off then as if preoccupied.

Tom and Jo were very pleased to leave with Mrs Kent but they were careful to keep their expressions neutral until they were in the car and away from their house.

The four teenagers then chatted non-stop for the entire trip. Gayle Kent ignored them with a smile. She knew that her twins were relieved that they would have friends at their new school.

Mrs Kent walked with all four of her passengers to the administration block.

"See you later, Wendy," Jo promised, and she walked with her brother towards their homeroom. Tom waved back at Will Kent.

They were in a very good mood as they walked away.

"Jo, Jackson and Tyson are over by the taps. Let's duck around behind the library!"

"Looks like they were waiting for us!" Jo commented. They would have had to pass them if they had walked to school. "And word seems to have got around!"

"What?" Tom asked, but then he noticed that other students were staring at them as they passed, and talking again after they had gone.

"Always wanted to be famous!" Tom grinned.

"Or infamous!" Jo joked back. She was amused because so many students that she did not know, recognised them, but at the same time she was unsettled, because it was the riff-raff that she usually tried to avoid that were smiling at them.

The relief they had felt the previous night when they had been told that they were not suspected of the robbery or the vandalism, and the delight of having Will and Wendy in their class, dissipated quickly once the day's routine began.

Rhodes insisted that they sit up the front during homeroom time and advised them that they were to be in the Seven Green homeroom during lunch. For the first time ever, the thought of detention irked.

They brightened up when their friends arrived and greeted them with smiles. Rhodes said nothing as Tom and Jo introduced their classmates to the new students. Julie and Mike, the only two students willing to sit next to Tom and Jo, quietly moved a space away to let the newcomers sit with their existing friends.

There was an audible groan when Rhodes announced a change of timetable for the morning. They were to have history, which they had missed the previous day, instead of a library period.

There was a lot more interest shown when Rhodes named the students from the class who would be competing in the following week's district sport's day. Tom and Jo were both on the school's team.

When the bell went, he wished the class a good day, collected his folders and said he would see everyone later for science.

Julie spoke across Wendy to Jo.

"I was told four times between the gate and here, that you and Tom robbed the canteen and sprayed the shed and that I had better lock my bag in my locker in case you nicked something from it."

Jo sighed. "The price of fame! You can ignore the sensational rumours. Yes, we had to clean up the mess in the shed, but no, we are not on the verge of being arrested, the police questioned us but they aren't stupid. They can't prove something we didn't do."

Julie looked relieved. Wendy made no comment, she had been advised not to let people know her father was the investigating officer, and she had warned Jo.

Julie dropped the subject and asked Wendy if she was good at sport.

"Not bad," Wendy grinned. "I like gymnastics and I jog a bit."

Wendy winked at Jo. "I think I could give Jo a run for her money!"

Julie grinned and Jo looked speculative.

"You're on, Wen!" Jo challenged. "We've got sport this arvo and PE on Friday!"

Jo raised her right hand when Wendy did and they smacked palms together.

"Sit down everyone!" Mrs Burgess said loudly, startling most of the class.

"Thomas, Josephine, I want you where I can see you."

Tom and Jo moved away from the groups they were in and returned to the seats nearest the teacher's desk.

Mrs Burgess then introduced herself to the two new students and added, "I'd advise you not to become involved with these two," she gestured at Tom and Jo, "they seem to be a bad influence."

The Kent twins gave no reaction.

When the class had settled, Mrs Burgess went to the front of the class and looked at Tom and Jo.

"I believe that two of you in this class have something to say to me?"

Tom glowered and Jo blushed.

The teacher remained looking expectantly at them.

Everyone in the class knew what she was waiting for and most of the students were feeling very uncomfortable.

Tom stood up.

"I apologise for my part in embarrassing you on Monday. I don't intend to do that again!"

As Tom sat down abruptly, Jo forced herself up.

"I'm sorry too, Mrs Burgess. I didn't realise it was you in the picture. It was meant to be funny for you too."

When Jo sat down again, she did not look at anyone and had to fight for control.

Mrs Burgess nodded, satisfied and began her lesson.

"Good man," Will Kent whispered in Tom's ear. He sensed Tom's anger and hoped to diffuse it.

Tom nodded, acknowledging that he had heard, but he too was continuing to look away from everyone. He wanted no one to see he was red faced.

Mrs Burgess gave the class a new assignment. Tom sat in silence, refusing to work. Jo made an effort to start, but kept glancing at her brother with concern. Finally, Tom returned her glance, noting that she was still red in the face and grinned at her. Jo grinned back. The shared grin made them both feel better.

"Having trouble with the questions, Thomas?"

"No, Miss," Tom answered with careful politeness. "I was just thinking about my answers first."

"A very good idea, something everyone should do," she commented neutrally, waiting for him to begin writing before moving away.

Tom relaxed a little. It seemed that Burgess was not going to hold a grudge.

As the class walked to the IT room for the following period, a small group of classmates surrounded Tom and Jo. The show of solidarity helped to ease their embarrassment. Their friends were vocal in their approval of their public apology and reminded that the joke had been an excellent one that had certainly livened things up.

The combination of the new students and their renewed popularity ensured that both Tom and Jo were in the middle of a group of students at the first break. The boys went off to play football and the girls took Wendy Kent on a tour of the school.

The presence of the group about each Dwyer, made it impossible for Fred Jackson to approach either of the Dwyers as he had intended. He wouldn't be able to do anything at lunchtime because he knew the Dwyers had detention. He'd have to act after school.

Toby Van Heuren, a slight brown haired boy in year eight, sidled up to his older brother, James at the end of recess.

"Jackson spent half the time following a bunch of girls around and the rest of the time watching football."

Toby raced off to his classroom and James reported the details to Mike Johnson who was collecting a variety of reports on Jackson's activities over the past few days. The reports came from his classmates or their siblings or friends in other classes. Ten Silver were rallying around two of their own, but so far nothing very useful had come to light.

The sport teacher treated Tom and Jo as normal. They had never misbehaved for him and his own judgement of their character had not changed. His only disgruntlement with them was that they refused to try out for the interschool sport teams. He was certain they would be an asset to any team.

Today he watched with amusement because Jo and the new girl had placed themselves in the same position on opposing netball teams and were obviously challenging each other. With a sigh, he thought to himself that if he could put both of them on the school's netball team — the team would be unbeatable.

Tyson watched the Dwyers retreating with the two new students and strode off to where Jackson was waiting by the back gate.

"They ain't coming, Fred," Tyson reported. "They're going off with the new kids."

Fred Jackson swore under his breath.

"What have they got tomorrow?" he asked Tyson.

"English, Geography, maths, PE, --- and music."

Chapter 7

"Why are you still here, Jo?" Helga Atkinson, the gym teacher, challenged.

Startled, Jo looked up briefly before returning to her systematic search of the seldom-used lockers in the girls changing room.

"Looking for my shoes!" Jo answered, sounding annoyed and slamming locker doors in her frustration.

She was dressed back in her normal uniform, except for her black shoes. They had been with her clothes before she went to the toilet. She said as much to her teacher.

"Perhaps someone picked them up by mistake?"

"Perhaps someone is wearing two pairs of shoes!" Jo retorted. "I don't have time for this. I have detention in five minutes and I still have to take this stuff to my locker and get my lunch and workbook."

Jo had not stopped searching. "Who was the sod who put them in here?"

The missing shoes were in one of the lowermost lockers, right at the back. She had to get on her hands and knees to see them.

"Why didn't your friends wait for you?" Atkinson asked.

"I told them not to, since I had another place to be. They'd gone before I discovered the shoes missing."

"Well, you had better hurry."

Jo did not need to be told. As much as she had enjoyed challenging Wendy Kent to keep her reputation as the best in the class at gym – this nasty prank had put her in a really foul mood. She could not imagine which of her classmates had been so mean. It was not a secret that she had detention. Everyone knew that being late for detention was not an option – unless you wanted an extra day of it.

Jo accepted detention because of the pranks she and Tom pulled – but she resented it when it wasn't of her doing.

Once out of the gymnasium, Jo raced over to the year ten locker room. She might just have time. Her homeroom was right next to it.

She shoved her sports bag into her coat locker and slammed it shut.

Before she could get her lunch and workbook from her book locker, she heard running footsteps and a year seven girl panted up to her.

"Are you Jo?"

Jo nodded.

"Julie told me to find you. Your brother is in a fight down behind the technology building – near the boys toilets."

"Thanks," Jo muttered, forgetting her lunch, books and detention and thinking only of stopping her brother from being in worse trouble that they were already. An extra day's detention was nothing compared to a week's suspension for fighting. She hoped to get there before the teachers did.

Jo raced out of the locker room and made for the technology block at her fastest pace. The tech block was in the furthest corner of the school and Jo was out of breath by the time she reached the nearest corner of it. It certainly sounded as if a fight was in progress.

She tried to run faster. There was scarcely time to realise that the noise was from a very rowdy game of touch ball – not a fight – when she was caught from behind. She had an arm put around her mouth, effectively gagging her and making it hard to catch her breath.

She struggled, desperately. All she could tell about those holding her were that they were tall enough to be in year 12 and that both faces were totally unfamiliar. In moments, she was bundled through a doorway and she realised that it was the boys' toilets.

Jo nearly panicked, but she recalled the lessons in self-defence that Ted had given her and prepared to act.

Before the arm was removed, one of the boys spoke to her.

"If you try to get attention, I'll hit you. We just want to talk to you. Understand?"

Jo nodded, terrified.

Her feet were put down and the arm stopped blocking her mouth. It was a relief to be able to draw a deep lungful of air. However, her right arm was grabbed and twisted up behind her. It hurt and she couldn't help groaning.

Fred Jackson came in. Jo managed to spit at him.

"What do you want?"

Jackson snarled at her.

"To get you and your brother for dobbing me in! I've got detention after school, all next week and the damn cops have been asking me questions."

"Serves you right, you maggot! You set us up, but we didn't tell Hendry it was you."

"Someone did and it wasn't me!" Jackson snarled back.

He drew out a water bottle from his jacket pocket and took a long swig. Then he threw the recapped bottle at one of the taller boys.

"You can let her have a drink, then shove her in a cubicle and keep her quiet. Keep everyone else out of here."

Jackson walked out – planning what he would do to get Tom Dwyer down here too.

Jo eyed the water bottle, but refused to ask for a drink. Her own bottle was in her gym bag and, after running here, her mouth was dry but she certainly didn't want to drink from a bottle Jackson had drunk from.

"Fred said drink!" the tall boy told Jo as he approached.

"Shove it up your rear!" Jo refused.

"We can arrange that," he offered with a crude laugh. "If you think it would improve the taste."

"Maggot!" Jo clamped her mouth shut as the boy uncapped the bottle and moved even closer. Thirsty or not, if they wanted her to drink, she wouldn't.

When the boy was close enough, she used the one holding her as a springboard, drew her knees up and kicked out. She pushed the boy back, but he managed to regain his balance without falling down. Unfortunately, she hadn't kicked him where it would hurt most and the water hadn't spilt.

All she achieved was to anger him. Seeing his determined look, Jo drew a deep breath to scream, but he was quick enough to shove the bottle into her mouth.

It wasn't water in the bottle but spirits of some kind she guessed. It burnt her throat and made her gag. The boy didn't remove the bottle and he was holding her mouth closed on it. A lot was spilling from the corners of her mouth, but she couldn't avoid swallowing some as she struggled to empty her mouth and to breathe.

It didn't take much thought to realize that they were trying to make her drunk. She remembered Ted telling her, repeatedly, to avoid getting so drunk that she didn't know what she was doing. But what did these boys intend to do to her?

Tom reached the detention room ahead of his sister. Wendy Kent had told him she wouldn't be long. He began to worry when the teacher arrived and Jo still hadn't.

Tom wasn't the only student in the room. There were two other boys that he only knew by sight.

The teacher checked his list of names and looked over his glasses at Tom.

"It seems that your sister doesn't wish to join us today," Reginald Church, one of the Year 12 specialist teachers, remarked. His tone was not forgiving.

"She was held up in PE," Tom said helplessly, glancing out the window and hoping to see her. If she arrived soon, Church might not give her an extra day of detention.

Tom fidgeted. This was not like his sister. She knew better.

"You are in here to work, Mister Dwyer," Church said. He had approached without Tom being aware of him and slammed his pointer onto the table.

Tom jumped and looked at the teacher's implacable face. He opened his workbook for English and tried to piece together an essay from the note's he had made. He began to write, but he was sure his efforts would be rubbish. His mind was wondering where Jo was and he kept glancing frequently out the window. Just before the bell, he spotted Fred Jackson loitering near the classroom.

Church blocked his way as he tried to leave.

"I haven't dismissed you, Dwyer," Church told Tom. He glanced in the direction of Tom's gaze and identified the boy.

"Sir, I have to find my sister. If she didn't come – something is wrong!"

"Very well," Church agreed, belatedly recalling the instruction to keep a special eye on Tom Dwyer and his sister.

"When you find her, tell her she has an extra two days detention. I will alert the staff to her absence."

Church stepped aside and let Tom out then gestures to the two other boys that they could leave.

"Hey, Dwyer!" Jackson called as Tom emerged.

"What is it?" Tom asked impatiently, as he made to walk past him.

"I know where your sister is."

"What have you done to her?"

"Me? Nothing! Come on."

Tom followed Fred Jackson across the quad yard and into the walk space under the tech block. He had to trot to keep up with Jackson's rapid walk.

"In here," Fred stopped and pushed on the door of the boy's toilets.

"Why would Jo be in here?" Tom asked suspiciously.

"You ask her – if you can get any sense out of her. If you ask me, she's too drunk to know where she is."

The only other person in the facility was Jo, who was sitting on a toilet seat, slumped against the side wall of the cubicle. Tom tried to wake her, and then tried to get her to stand up. She was like jelly – totally unable to walk. He rested her back on the seat.

"You did it!" Tom accused the smirking Jackson.

"Not I," Jackson denied. "Though she is wearing nice frilly knickers and bra!"

Tom, already angry, took a swing at the smirking face. Jackson blocked it.

"Nice tits too," he goaded further.

Tom lost his temper completely and threw punch after punch at Jackson. He pushed the other boy into the wall and occasionally hit him. Jackson defended himself, laughing at Tom but not hitting back. The laughter infuriated Tom further and Jackson was pleased with his set up. They were making enough noise that someone would come soon.

The timing could not have been better. The door was flung open at the exact instant Tom landed a punch on Jackson's nose, causing it to bleed.

Two year-twelve boys, from the classroom next to the toilets, barged in and separated the combatants; Tom tried to continue the fight by kicking out at Fred as he was dragged back.

A third year twelve boy entered the facility while a fourth went off to report to their teacher.

"Dwyer! Stop it!" the latest arrival snapped.

Sanity returned to Tom.

"He got my sister drunk. She's down in the cubicle. And he's been touching her!" Tom shouted, trying to struggle free.

Fred shook his head.

"He's got it in for me. I was only trying to help keep her out of trouble by telling him where I found her."

The senior boys took in the damage to Jackson's face and the lack of marks on Tom.

"What do you think, Kel?" the boy holding Tom asked of the third boy.

"I'm not going to sort it out," Kelly Phillips, the school captain proclaimed. "Jim will be back with one of the teachers, they can handle it."

Phillips strode over to the open cubicle and stared in at Jo for a moment. The reek of some kind of spirit was still strong. There was a bottle on the floor, rolled partway under the wall to the next cubicle. He picked the bottle up and sniffed the opening. The former water bottle reeked of the alcohol.

Phillips tried to animate Jo too. She seemed aware of him but her eyes were unfocussed and her voice was slurred. All he could be sure that she was saying was, "I feel sick."

That wasn't surprising; she looked terrible. It looked like she had brought it on herself though. He felt no pity, only disgust and he left Jo sitting where she was.

Phillips knew the type of person that Jackson was and had heard too much about Tom and Jo Dwyer lately. If that pair were trying to be like

Jackson, they needed to be taught better. He stood up straighter as the first of the teachers summoned by Jim entered the facility.

Hendry the Vice Principal entered ahead of Scott, the Principal.

Phillips recognised a lack of humour in Hendry that matched Scott's normal state.

"Get them out of here," Scott told the senior boys, his tone glacial.

"Sir," Phillips nodded his head in Jo's direction.

Scott strode over to the cubicle and stared in disgust.

"Get her to the nurse," he ordered. "This sort of behaviour won't be tolerated."

Scott strode out and headed back to the admin building.

Fred Jackson and Tom Dwyer were already being hustled in the same direction. Tom was struggling because he wanted to help his sister.

Hendry went into the cubicle and tried to talk to Jo.

"What happened, Jo?" he asked gently, squatting down to watch her face.

Phillips was surprised at his concern. Jo tried to struggle upright.

"I din, dint wan t' dink," Jo tried to speak properly but could not control her mouth. It was fuzzy, numb.

"Can you walk?" Hendry asked, and watched as Jo tried again unsuccessfully to push herself up. Even with support on both sides, her legs were like rubber – with no strength in them.

With the support of the senior student and teacher, Jo managed to stumble into the school's infirmary. Phillips went to find the school nurse, who would have just gone off to lunch. Hendry helped Jo to lie down on the bed, and then waited for the nurse to return.

Kelly Phillips went back to his class and Hendry answered the nurse's questions.

"She might have quite a lot in her system already," the nurse decided. "Leave her with me. I'll give you a report later."

Hendry returned to his office, as the nurse went to prepare the treatment for her patient.

Jo had enough awareness left to know she was feeling dreadful. But the nurse gave her something to drink, something vile, and she immediately threw up into the bowl the nurse had provided her.

When the retching ceased, Jo began to shiver and could not stop her eyes streaming water.

A blanket was placed around her and the bowl removed. Jo hugged the blanket tighter and was grateful to comply with the suggestion that she lie down. She was also thankful that the nurse was not lecturing her about the state she was in. She wished she could remember what had happened.

Tom Dwyer received the full fury of the Principal's tongue-lashing. Scott asked him what had caused the fight and why he was hitting the other boy when the other was restraining himself.

Tom wished himself elsewhere; anywhere but where he was. He had started the fight. He had lost his temper and even if Jackson had provoked him, he should not have hit him. The Principal was perfectly correct to be censuring him. That was not the worst part. Jackson had known exactly how to manipulate him and had set him up again.

Anger surged through Tom at the thought of Jackson's actions. He answered the Principals scathing questions with an impolitic tactlessness that did not endear him to the man.

Having to admit his guilt was worse that apologising to the history teacher in front of the whole class. He felt lower that a cockroach in the shadow of someone's boot.

Scott left Tom alone; once he was sure his message had sunk in. It gave Tom time to worry about his sister. They may not be twins, but they were as close as if they were.

The door to the principal's office was still open, but Tom stayed where he was, aware that anyone coming near the office would see him and know of his utter disgrace. He felt his face growing hot. How was he going to face his classmates? How was he going to face Ted?

A murmur of voices coming from nearby grew louder. Tom hoped Jackson was getting the 'High Lecture' too. It was small consolation.

Hendry came into Scott's office.

"You are to get your backpack from your locker and return here. I will have someone collect your other books from your homeroom."

Tom nodded and stood up, wondering why Hendry himself was

shepherding him. He walked in silence, the breeze outside cooling his face.

At the locker room, Tom dragged his backpack out of his coat locker. His water bottle fell out as he tried to right it. Hendry retrieved the bottle, twisted off the cap and sniffed the contents. He didn't give it to Tom who was putting books from his book locker into his bag with hands that were visibly trembling.

An envelope fell out. Again, Hendry retrieved the object. It contained money, lots of it.

"Tom?" Hendry queried the student.

Tom's face went very pale and he slumped against his locker.

"Sir, I haven't any idea what that's from or where it came from."

Hendry did not doubt him. Tom Dwyer was completely subdued; he had no trace of rebellion or resistance left.

"When you've finished packing your bag, will you help me with your sister's?"

"Yes, Sir," Tom agreed dully.

Hendry had a master key for the lockers and Tom knew which was Jo's.

Tom packed what he thought he and his sister would need during what he knew would be an enforced absence from school. Hendry stood by, waiting quietly.

"Does your sister bring a water bottle like yours to school?" Hendry asked carefully.

"Yes, Sir." Tom answered without even wondering why he wanted to know.

"Is it here?"

"Not in her locker, Sir. It might be in her gym bag."

Hendry felt the soft fabric bag that had been in Jo's coat locker. He found the shape of a bottle and opened the bag enough to remove it. As he had done with Tom's, he sniffed the contents. The bottle was almost empty, but it smelt like water. He put the bottle back. It was identical to the one that had been found with Jo. It wasn't conclusive — many of the students used and reused those purchased water bottles.

Chapter 8

Tom slumped on the bench outside Scott's office. He roused from his funk when he heard voices getting louder. One was Scott's and he knew the other. It wasn't Ted and it wasn't Uncle Ed, thank heavens. He wished he could shrink or hide.

Inspector Kent, Tom realised. Hell! He didn't look amused, or friendly. He looked official. What was he doing there?

Kent only glanced at Tom as he was ushered into Scott's office and the door was closed.

Tom watched the door. After a while he realised that he could see into Hendry's office to where Jackson was seated. Jackson must have seen Kent too. He looked worried, at least until he saw Tom watching him. Then he forced a smirk. Tom returned a mirthless grin, which changed Jackson's smirk to a scowl.

Kent went into Hendry's office and was in there for a while. The door was closed during that time, but Jackson emerged shortly before the bell was due to ring. He had a letter protruding from his pocket and a smirk firmly in place on his face.

"Cheers," Fred greeted. "I've got detention on Monday, thanks to you!"

"Poor baby," Tom insulted the other boy. "I'm betting I'll get a week's holiday."

Tom felt a ripple of amusement that enabled him to give the impression that he welcomed suspension.

"I'm not finished with you!" Jackson said in a low growl. He walked off before he was noticed talking to Tom. He actually had an extra week's detention, not just Monday, and he had been officially warned by the policeman to stay away from Tom and Jo Dwyer.

Tom sank back into apathy when Jackson had gone. It wasn't fair. No, it was fair, but it wasn't his fault.

"Tom."

Inspector Kent stood in front of him.

"Sir," Tom answered, standing up.

"I'm taking you home. Collect your things and we will go to get Jo. Will can bring your things from your home room and any work you have to do."

"Yes, Sir," Tom agreed, picking up his pack and Jo's. He led the way to the infirmary.

"Why are you taking us home?" Tom asked after a while. "I thought that Ted would have to come."

"I didn't give Constable Dwyer permission to go off duty," Kent told Tom. "He was needed where he was and I wanted to reinforce in certain minds that the police are taking an active interest in matters here."

"I don't need that reminder," Tom said sourly.

"I wasn't meaning you. I tried to get Scott to give you a week's detention – like young Jackson got – but he wouldn't. He doesn't intend to make exceptions. It means that you won't be able to compete in the district sports next week either."

Tom shrugged, accepting that.

"Thank you for trying, Sir. It was good of you."

"I've warned Fred Jackson to stay away from you," Kent went on. "And I am giving you the same warning. Keep away from him and his mates."

"I'll promise to try very hard," Tom agreed. It could be difficult.

"I'll ask Will to stick with you," Kent suggested.

"Is he going to get detention too, to keep me company?"

"I hope not!"

Kent's response drew a faint grin from Tom.

"I'll still have two lunch time detentions when I get back," Tom told the police officer. "Jo got two extra for missing today."

"I believe that Jackson will be occupied after school for the next two weeks. One for inciting you to skip class and another for this afternoon."

"No wonder he said he hadn't finished with me," Tom said without thinking.

Kent stopped and turned Tom to face him.

"He said that did he?"

Tom nodded. "Just before you came out and got me."

"Perhaps a week's suspension isn't such a bad thing," Kent mused.

Tom didn't mention that Jackson had a long memory.

Jo was sitting up and seemed better than she had been an hour ago, but she still looked miserable. Her eyes were red and watery.

"Mr Scott told me you were taking us home," Jo managed to say with only slight slurring of her voice. "I suppose it's better than everyone thinking we are being arrested. Not everyone knows that our brother is a policeman."

"Yes indeed," Kent agreed mildly. He didn't mention that he had considered that himself.

"Are you ready to leave?"

Jo nodded and eased herself off the bed. She still wasn't steady on her feet but in spite of a tendency to weave from side to side, she made it out to the Inspector's car without needing support.

"You got the 'High Lecture' too," Tom remarked as they settled into the back seat of the car.

"Yeah."

"And the week's suspension?"

"Yeah, and the extra two days detention for missing one. It's not fair."

"You didn't have to come after me," Tom said. It wasn't really a suggestion. She wouldn't leave him to trouble, any more than he would her. "Jackson has two weeks of detention. I'd rather the holiday."

"But it means being home with Him!" Jo pointed out. Tom glanced at Kent in the driver's seat, but he seemed to be concentrating on the traffic.

As if he had heard them, Kent drove them to his own house and left them with his wife. She asked no questions of her husband and worked quietly to put her guests at ease. She soon had them confiding in her the events of the day. Jo began to remember what had happened after PE.

Gayle Kent was horrified by what she heard and questioned Jo to try to determine if she had been molested by the boys.

Tom told Jo what Jackson had claimed. Jo actually giggled, with relief.

"That's not what I've got on," she assured her brother. "Not on a sport day or for PE!"

Tom relaxed a little, but felt like a worse idiot for believing Jackson.

"I wish I knew who those other two boys were. The ones doing Fred's dirty work. They had uniforms on – but I'm sure I've never seen them before."

Tom and Jo both felt better after a light snack and some peace and quiet. They decided to stay where they were when Mrs Kent left to go pick up her own children.

On their return, William came barrelling into the living room.

"Hiya, pal!" he said cheerfully to Tom. "Hi Jo!"

"Why are you so chirpy?" Tom asked sourly. "Are you celebrating our disgrace?"

"Na! It's Friday! No school for two whole days. Lucky dog! No school for you for nine days."

"William Kent!" his mother scolded him. "Don't you even consider getting suspended for a week off."

"Aw, Mum!" he protested, winking at Tom. "Actually, Pal, the whole class is behind you. Especially since Jackson was loudly telling his mates about you being suspended and why. He's got a beaut black nose. We all decided he was behind it because Rhodes didn't mention anything to us."

"Well he was, even if he didn't soil his hands," Tom stated.

"Unfortunately for you, however," Wendy added when she walked in with her mother, "Rhodes sent a pile of worksheets home for you to do."

Tom groaned.

"And Mum's going to call your Aunt and tell her you are here. We'll take you home after your brother gets off duty."

"Dad's home," Wendy announced, hearing a car door slam out in the street. A second car door closed, so Wendy peeked out through the curtain. "Your brother is here too."

"Does he look mad?" Jo asked.

"He's talking to dad. I can't tell."

"I said, keep out of it, Constable!" they heard Inspector Kent saying as the two men entered. "If you get involved, I'll have you step down."

"They're my family. I'm responsible for them." Ted was arguing.

"We'll discuss this later, Constable," Kent silenced his guest.

Ted glanced into the front room and saw Tom and Jo. They stood up and went to greet him. Kent beckoned to his children and they followed him through to the kitchen.

Ted reassured his siblings by taking them into a big hug.

"You idiots," he said, betraying how anxious he'd been. "Jo, are you sure you are alright?"

"Yes, but I feel totally lousy. Do you know we got suspended?"

Ted nodded. "I can't fault your loyalty to each other – but as things stand, you will have to be more careful and take someone with you."

"There wasn't time," Jo said.

"No, he arranged it well," Ted agreed. "He didn't let you think first. Tom, next time, try to restrain yourself."

"What would you have done," Tom asked quietly.

"Probably the same," Ted admitted, also quietly.

Tom recalled the snippet of conversation they had heard as Ted had come in and wondered what Ted had been censured for.

Jo told her brother what she had remembered since being away from school. Ted's expression was unreadable.

"Kent thinks you should stay here this week. Would you prefer that?" Ted asked.

Tom and Jo nodded, guiltily.

"I'll tell him. But don't think you are going to have a holiday. Kent is a fair man but he won't tolerate nonsense. You'll have to do the work your school sent home."

Tom looked away. "Fair enough," he agreed.

"You'll have to go home tonight though. I have some things I have to do there. I'll tell Uncle what's going on."

"Do you have to?" Jo asked. "He'll be insufferable."

"No reason not to," Ted countered. He was debating about whether to mention the real reason.

Edward Dwyer was about to leave for work when Ted, Tom and Jo returned home.

"I thought these two were grounded. They should've been home hours ago," Dwyer's voice was threatening.

"Bed!" Ted told Tom and Jo who had agreed to act subdued on their return.

Ted watched as they went meekly upstairs and commented to his Uncle.

"The little idiots got themselves suspended for a week."

"They're out of control, Son," Edward Dwyer said solicitously. "A good hiding is what they need."

"No," Ted said quite mildly. "I think this has finally got through to them."

"Well, I can keep an eye on them during the day," Ed Dwyer promised.

"It's good of you, Uncle, but what about when you are at work? You can't expect Aunt Hilda to watch them. Kent has offered to have them for the week, I agreed. It will not be a holiday. Kent won't tolerate nonsense and tricks and he'll be a subtle reminder, all week, as to what will happen if they don't stop misbehaving."

Ed Dwyer snorted with amusement. "Subtle! Good enough. I wouldn't like to be under his eye. They didn't like his attention the other night did they? Perhaps that's what brought this on."

Ted shrugged. "Who knows? I can't remember being that stupid as a teenager. Anyway, Uncle, I will be staying here, but Kent is sending me up bush for four days from next Tuesday. I'll be leaving Monday night, back Saturday."

Chapter 9

Ted Dwyer returned home to an empty house and wondered where his Uncle and Aunt were. He rang the Kent's place, told Tom he was back and that he would be over to pick them up in an hour.

Just then, he heard the front door open and his aunt come in. She had a suitcase with her and she was wearing her coat. Ted helped her out of the coat and took the case into her room. She didn't share with Uncle.

"How have you been, Aunt?" he asked, giving her a brief kiss on the cheek.

"I've been visiting my sister," Hilda Dwyer enthused. "I have a lot of new patterns for cushion covers. It would have been nice to stay longer. I haven't visited her for so long but your Uncle insisted I be back for when Tom and Jo get back."

"And where is Uncle?"

"He's got work on a trawler- a week or ten days, perhaps."

Hilda Dwyer was used to her husband's frequent absences. She went through to the kitchen to make a cup of tea.

"Oh, dear!" Ted heard her say and he followed her to see what prompted the remark.

Over a dozen beer glasses and twice that of empty bottles were stacked in and around the sink. The ashtrays on the kitchen table were full of dozens of butts.

"Men can be so helpless," Hilda sighed and began cleaning up the mess.

Ted helped by emptying the ashtrays and carting the bottles out to the recycle bin. He had other ideas about 'helpless'. Lazy, was more like it. At least all the mess was in one room and his uncle did not have his cronies over when his sister and brother were around.

Tom and Jo looked well and seemed more relaxed than they had been before he left. They were happy to hear that their uncle would be away for another week.

"Ted, I know that you agreed with Uncle about being grounded for two weeks," Jo began in a wheedling voice. "And it isn't quite up yet, but can we please go bike riding with Will and Wendy tomorrow? They'll let us use their old bikes. Please, please, please."

"Does their father agree to this?" Ted asked before committing himself.

"He suggested it," Jo told him. "But you had to agree. We will only be going as far Henty Park. They have bike tracks all through there and we will probably be stopping for a drink at the shops on the way back."

"Have you been good?" Ted asked sternly.

"Of course we have," Jo claimed. "We did all the work the school sent home for us and Wendy said Rhodes was impressed. Auntie Gayle will drop us back home."

"Ok, you can go. Uncle won't be around to say anything. Too bad if he was."

Neither Tom nor Jo had ever been to Henty Park, so Will and Wendy paid for a tour of the old house there. The tour was organised by the historical group who were slowly restoring the house. The kitchen and master bedroom had been restored and the tour even went through the secret passage that joined those two rooms. The visitors were allowed to draw their own conclusions as to why the original owner had built it.

There were cellars under the kitchen, but they were not considered to be safe, so the tour did not go down there.

It was a fascinating visit and being a sunny day, riding around the park was a pleasure. All four teenagers were ready for a drink when they reached the shops.

Will went to buy them, whilst the other three took over a table and four chairs in an outside seating area.

Whilst they were drinking the milkshakes, the four teenagers talked of inconsequential things. During a break in the conversation, Tom heard a snippet of conversation in a voice that sounded like his Uncle's. He looked up and saw another group of people, two tables away. A man, with his back to him, was wearing a suit.

Jo followed her brother's glance and something about the man sent shivers down her spine. Her hand grabbed her brother's wrist and she mouthed the word "Uncle" at him.

Tom shook his head. How could it be?

"He's wearing the same suit as he had on the day he came to school," Jo whispered fiercely. "There is a mended tear on the back near the right sleeve."

"Is this discussion private?" Will Kent asked, feeling ignored.

"No, but it's stupid," Tom said in a low voice. "The man two tables away, not the big one, the shorter, stockier one, looks like uncle dressed up – but he's meant to be away on a fishing boat."

Tom moved carefully so he wasn't looking directly towards the big man.

"I've never seen your Uncle," Wendy commented. "What if I go over to the toilet block and try for a look at him on the way back?"

Tom and Jo nodded and kept their heads down. Within five minutes, Wendy was back.

"Let's go," she said quietly, but with such seriousness that the others obeyed at once.

They left their empty drink containers on the table, and quietly wheeled their bikes down the road a bit before mounting.

After they had travelled about half a mile, Wendy turned off the main road and stopped.

"What was that about? Will asked his sister.

"I got a good look at the two men. I'll know them both again, but the big man – I'm sure that he's Fred Jackson's father. I'm sure I've seen the woman before too."

"How do you know it is Fred's father?" Jo asked.

"I had to go up to the school office, last week, to give them our reports from our last school. I saw him with Fred, talking to Hendry."

"Wendy has a good memory for faces. Even dad says so," Will claimed. "And if that wasn't Fred himself that just rode by, I'll become a monk."

"And stop trying to get Julie to go out with you," Wendy teased. "He's got a crush on her," she whispered to Jo.

"If it was Uncle and Jackson," Tom said slowly, "And Fred was following us – does that mean he saw us?"

"I'm not waiting to find out!" Jo decided. "Is there another way to get back to your place?"

"Yeah," Will told them. "Come on."

The four teenagers arrived back at the Kent house without any further sightings of Fred Jackson. They still weren't sure if the man they'd seen was their Uncle. All they had to go on was the mend in the jacket.

Tom and Jo decided to mention it to Ted, mainly because Fred Jackson might have been following them. Ted thought it couldn't have been their Uncle, but he made some enquiries.

"Uncle's car is parked behind the cannery, I checked with the company. He is out on the UQV, one of their trawlers as acting first mate. It can't have been him," Ted told his siblings later.

Tom and Jo still were not convinced either way but had to accept the facts Ted had discovered.

It was odd being back at school after the week off, but everyone accepted their presence as if they had not been away. Devin Rhodes even praised them for their work.

Rhodes watched Tom and Jo carefully during his lesson and was satisfied by what he saw. They were working quietly, cooperatively and finishing the work on time. Other teachers who took Ten Silver were finding the same. He hoped they had finally learnt their lesson. They finished their lunchtime detentions without fuss and Rhodes hoped the state of affairs would last. He did not realise that Fred Jackson was inexplicably absent all that first week that Tom and Jo were back.

"Tell him Spiv rang. I'm a packet short," the harsh voice on the phone ordered.

Jo agreed to pass on the message. She shivered as she put the receiver down. She had answered the phone, expecting it to be from Wendy Kent, but the man had wanted her Uncle and had not been pleased to learn that Eddy was not due back for several more days.

Jo did not know what to make of the message, and was sure she did not want to write it down for her Uncle. Instead, she made a mental note to tell her Aunt of the call and have her pass the message on. She would be back in half an hour.

Jo went upstairs to Tom's room and knocked twice on the door. She entered immediately, and caught Tom hiding a magazine under his pillow.

"Damn, Sorry. I thought you were Aunt Hilda."

"What are you hiding?" Jo asked.

Tom sheepishly pulled out a magazine full of naked women.

"I found it amongst the papers I had to put out. I bet Aunt Hilda put it there," Tom admitted.

"Uncle better not catch you with it" Jo warned.

"You don't need to tell me," Tom agreed. "I'll slip it out to the bin later. What's up with you?"

"I just answered the phone. It was someone wanting Uncle."

Jo told her brother the message.

"You're right, you had better convince Aunt to pretend she took the message. He'll go ballistic if he thinks we know something about his business."

"Oh, I agree," Jo said. "But I had an idea. You know how Aunt complained about the mess she had to clean up when she got back – obviously, Uncle had his mates over. What would Uncle give them by the packet – several packets? He's too stingy to give anything away."

"He'd sell stuff," Tom mused. "What do you reckon? Something small that might have been dropped and kicked under something? Is that what you are suggesting?"

Jo nodded.

"Do you really want to know?" Tom asked.

"Aunt is not here. Uncle won't be back for a day or two. I think he's up to something. What better chance?"

It wasn't often that they were home by themselves. Their uncle was paranoid about the privacy of his den. The temptation was irresistible.

The door was locked, but Jo knew where her Aunt kept a spare key.

She went quickly into her Aunt's room and took it from her jewellery box. Uncle's den was downstairs and the key opened the lock easily.

Tom and Jo crept in slowly, not without a sense of danger. They were almost afraid that their uncle would suddenly appear. The room was in its usual state of mess, but they didn't intend to touch anything, they were merely looking.

Jo knelt down and looked under the chairs, Tom reached an arm under the couch and felt around. He pulled out a small brown paper wrapped packet. He showed it to Jo.

The brown paper had clear tape around it, so they dared not try to open it, but then they noticed one corner was torn slightly and they opened it a little bit more. Inside was a wad of reddish orange paper, the exact colour of twenty-dollar bills.

Tom dropped the packet as if it were a live snake and kicked it back under the couch. "Let's get out of here."

Jo needed no urging and locked the door after them.

Chapter 10

Next morning they went down to breakfast and found their uncle had returned. Hiding their surprise and without greeting him, they fetched their own breakfasts and sat at the far end of the table from him. Apart from giving them a quick glance, he ignored them and continued reading his paper.

Aunt Hilda entered a few minutes later and was reminded about the phone message by seeing Jo.

"Edward, dear, there was a message for you…"

"Shut your trap!" Dwyer told his wife. "Tell me later."

Jo hated having her Aunt treated that way and changed the subject.

"What time did Ted get back last night?"

"He came in about five this morning," Hilda Dwyer told Jo.

"Oh!" was her disinterested sounding reply.

It meant that they wouldn't be able to talk to him about what they had seen until late afternoon.

"You two had better get the paper stuff out before you go to school," Dwyer told his niece and nephew.

"Yes, Uncle," Tom agreed readily. "It's all ready. I tied it up last night."

Jo decided her uncle looked surprised and wondered if this was a way they might use to subtly annoy him.

They were going back to get the last load of papers when they heard their uncle calling them in a very polite manner.

"Tom, Jo, your ride is here."

"They're early," Jo commented as they carried the piles to the front and stacked them in the box.

Wendy was at the front door chatting to their uncle.

"Hurry up you two. Dad's dropping us off today," she chivvied them.

"Just get my bag," Tom promised, as he trotted inside to get it.

"Don't take all day," Wendy called. "You may not want to get there for history, but I don't want to be late."

"Alright, alright," Jo muttered, going inside.

"They don't like history," Wendy confided in Edward Dwyer. "Mrs Burgess made them apologise to her in front of the whole class."

Edward Dwyer chuckled.

"At least there is someone at that school that can make them behave."

Tom and Jo returned quickly and walked to the Inspector's car. Dwyer watched them leave before returning inside.

"Good morning," Inspector Kent greeted them. "Keeping out of trouble?"

"Not all the time."

Jo decided in that instant, to tell him about the phone call yesterday and what they'd done and seen.

The Inspector listened, thoughtfully.

"Tom, Jo, I want you to promise me that you will not attempt to spy on your uncle."

"Why?" Jo asked.

"Because he could be dangerous," was the warning from the policeman. "Wendy, what's your opinion?"

"Jo, you know how we thought you thought you saw your uncle last week? I went up to the door to get you so that I could see your uncle close up."

"How did you know he was home?"

"Your brother traced his car. We've had a discrete watch on it," Kent revealed. "He was followed home."

Wendy continued, "I'm convinced the bloke we saw was him. The eyes and the hair colour are the same and the difference in style is nothing."

"What are you implying," Tom asked intently.

"Nothing yet," Kent cautioned. "He may simply be two timing your aunt. However, what you saw in his den concerns me, especially in the light of the break in at your school. We started checking your uncle because of his connection with Stan Jackson who has had several past convictions and because Fred Jackson seems to be trying to get you both in strife."

"Does Ted know?" Jo asked.

"Some of it. I will tell him what you saw and Wendy's conclusions. Just remember this may be nothing."

"He's hardly God's gift to women," Tom muttered.

"Just keep out of trouble!" Kent warned them. "Has the Jackson boy been annoying you?"

"He hasn't been to school," Tom was pleased to report.

"Tom, try to keep with Will and Jo, try to keep with Wendy"

Kent's serious tone convinced Tom and Jo to decide to obey him.

Edward Dwyer strode inside once the police car had disappeared down the street.

He spared a moment to wonder why the girl had chosen to come to the door to get Tom and Jo this time. Although he had not betrayed the fact, he recognised her from the weekend before last and Stan Jackson's boy had identified her and spotted Tom and Jo. They seemed to have no idea they had been seen and can't have identified him.

However, he'd had the sense of being followed home last night and the boys at the cannery had noticed that his car was being watched.

"Hilda, what was that message?" he called after he had closed the door.

"Some man called and said he was a packet short," Hilda told him, not mentioning that Jo had taken the message.

"Who was it?" her husband insisted impatiently.

"Sounded like Spiv." Hilda told him. "I might have heard wrong!"

"That would be right. Did he say anything else?"

"No," Hilda said, sniffing. "Rude, he was!"

Dwyer had some urgent matters to see to and he did not want potential witnesses. He pulled out a wad of money and pulled off two hundred dollars.

"Why don't you go and buy yourself a new outfit, Hilda darling. And think about where you would like to go out to tea."

Hilda's eyes lit up, but she stifled all curiosity about what prompted the gesture. He wanted her out of the way, probably intended to have his mates over again. Well, she would stay out until just before Tom and Jo were due back. She wasted no time getting her bag and walking to the bus stop.

Edward Dwyer went into his den and looked around carefully. He kept it untidy, deliberately. The mess had a purpose. He could tell at a glance if someone had been in there moving stuff around and spying on him. He never left anything incriminating in there, well, except for last night and that package was dynamite. If the police found that on him, he would be gaoled for sure. That is why he had it – it would have been more dangerous if he had taken it to his warehouse. He did not want to be associated with it in his identity as Edward Dwyer. The package would have to go – fast.

The package Spiv was missing was not as dangerous, but almost. If certain busy bodies found it, the police would come sniffing around.

He wouldn't be able to keep deceiving Ted into thinking he was a law-abiding citizen. Having a policeman living in his house was excellent camouflage and the only reason he tolerated the presence of his nephews and niece.

Dwyer recalled where he had moved the table to sort and pack the fake twenties he'd printed. Spiv, the skinny Italian, had been sitting on the couch. Dwyer knelt down and looked under it. It was too dark to see anything so he went out to the hall cupboard and grabbed the dolphin torch.

In the beam of light from the torch, Dwyer saw a package right at the back, touching the wall. He cursed Spiv for not counting his packages before he left.

Dwyer did not try to move the couch; it was too heavy. Built into it was a safe made of solid steel. Instead, he stretched his brawny arm under the couch and grabbed the parcel. As he drew his arm out, a lot of dust and rubbish and a pale blue button came with it.

He examined the package and saw that the corner was torn, revealing the contents.

He stalked to the phone, the extension he had put in his den, and dialled a mobile number from memory.

"Get over here, you moron," he told Spiv. "If you want that packet you left here, you have a job to do."

"Yeah, right. I've already paid for it," Spiv argued.

"The packet was partly opened. You don't open it until you are away!"

"Didn't touch it!" Spiv asserted. "Why'd I need to?"

"Just get over here! Wait in my den – careful though, my nephew is here asleep."

Spiv agreed. He wanted the 'money' he'd bought.

Dwyer idly replaced the receiver and let his eyes scan the room. It didn't look disturbed, but his eyes returned to the pale blue button and he bent swiftly to pick it up.

Blue, like Tom's school shirt.

"Damn kids," he muttered and without waiting for Spiv to arrive, he strode out the front door, locked it and went to his car. He wasted no time getting in and revved the engine harder than normal, before easing out into the street.

If Tom or his sister had found that money, they would blab to Ted. Maybe not to the other cop, but definitely to Ted.

Spiv didn't like cops, he kept saying about removing his bastard nephew. He wouldn't need to be told what to do if Ted took it into his head to check on what his ratty younger sibs claimed.

All being well, Ted would stay asleep, the evidence would be gone and no one would be able to prove anything. Ted thought his sibs were little liars anyway – but he might feel obliged to check.

Ted woke, hearing a car start up. He got out of bed and watched through the window as his uncle drove off. Automatically, he glanced at the time – nine o'clock. He wasn't due back on duty until one o'clock.

Still in his sleep shorts, he crossed from his room to the toilet and then decided to take a shower. He was just towelling himself dry when the phone rang. He walked to the hall to answer it.

"Dwyer, Kent here. Jo and Tom told me that they saw a brown paper wrapped packet in your uncle's den. They believe it contained money, a wad of twenties. They kicked it back under the couch. Is your uncle there?"

"No, he went off about ten or fifteen minutes ago – like the devil was after him."

"He had a call about a missing packet, Jo told me," Kent went on. "We are probably too late – he must have found it."

"Well, he's not here. It won't take me long to check."

"Be careful, we don't want to spook him if he's involved. I'm on my way over."

Ted finished drying himself and threw the towel in the laundry basket. In his room, he threw on a t-shirt and shorts. With a faint grin, he remembered Jo telling him where there was a spare key to his uncles den, though if he was in such a hurry, he may not have locked it. He would check that first.

Ted tried the door of the den, which was at the back of the house on the lower floor. It opened, so Ted walked into the threshold and looked around. There was a package on the table; brown paper wrapped. He went over and began to lift it. It was too heavy to contain money.

That was all he had time to think about when his world went black.

Spiv lowered the torch with a feeling of satisfaction. That was one cop that wasn't going anywhere. To make sure, Spiv grabbed a roll of wide sticky tape from off the table, the same stuff they had used to wrap the money packets, and wound it around the cop's mouth, eyes and wrists. As an afterthought, he wrapped some around the cop's ankles too. The cop began to stir, so Spiv threw a rug from the couch over his face.

Spiv pulled out his mobile phone and dialled a number so he could report to Eddy Dwyer, who he also knew of as Eddy Dawson.

"Eddy, Spiv. There was a phone call, and then yer ruddy nephew poked his nose in yer den. He saw a packet that you had left on the table – was about to open it so I decked him. What do you want me to do?"

Dwyer swore vilely. He automatically patted the pocket where he thought he had put that parcel, but felt only the packet of money. He remembered then that he had removed the plates before he crawled on the floor. Being followed home yesterday had really rattled him. The plates were for ten dollar notes and he'd paid a small fortune for them.

Dwyer took a deep breath, so when he spoke to Spiv he sounded perfectly calm.

"Drag him out to the shed, and lock the door." Dwyer ordered. "Bring the parcel with you. Be very careful with it, damage it and I will permanently damage you. There may be more cops on the way, so wait behind the shed. I will drive into the alley that touches my place in that corner. When you hear me, if it is safe, toss the big bundle over and then come over yourself. If the cops get there first, get over yourself and I will pick you up."

Edward Dwyer breathed a sigh of relief. That had been too close.

"What yer goin' ter do with him?" Spiv asked. "Take him to work?"

"No, too risky in daylight. We'll take him to the warehouse for now."

"You're squeamish, Dwyer," Spiv spat. "I'd kill the bastard."

"His mates will be buzzing enough if he's missing. I can't risk them turning up and he might still be useful. We don't have time to do a proper job right now – I'll have to get back and do damage control."

Dwyer had seen a police car pulling up outside his house as he drove past his street. Most likely it was the Inspector who had picked up his niece and nephew. The brats must have blabbed to him, probably trying to get on his good side and trying to cause trouble too.

Dwyer sped up a bit to get around to the entrance of the lane way. It backtracked to dogleg behind his house. He drove slowly as he neared his place and opened the door quietly before whistling the signal he'd developed to alert his mates at the docks. Spiv answered with the danger signal, and moments later, a large tarp wrapped bundle had fallen over the fence. As Dwyer hefted the bundle into the boot of his car, the slight wiry figure of Spiv landed gently on the ground in the lane.

"The cops are here," he warned.

The car doors were only lightly latched as the car moved slowly along the second half of the alley. They did not wish to be heard by the police at the house.

Spiv, might be a slightly built Italian, but he was as strong as an ox. He carried the again unconscious cop into one of the small storerooms at the warehouse. The car had been driven right inside the building and the roller door closed again before they had unloaded the boot. Ted had been stirring, so Spiv had knocked him on the head again.

Dwyer took the small package from Spiv and walked up the stairs to his office above the warehouse floor. Once it was locked away in his safe he breathed a sigh of relief, but the danger wasn't over yet. He walked back to Spiv.

"Here's your packet! Be more careful next time and forget you saw me today!"

Spiv wasted no time departing, allowing Dwyer to back his car out and relock the door. The Italian was one of a very small group who knew that Dwyer had an interest in this warehouse, but he only thought Dwyer was renting it. In fact, he owned it under the name of Dixon. A lot more people knew Eddy Dwyer as Eddy Dawson of Dawson Imports – the company that owned the building next door.

Dwyer quickly returned to his car and drove off. He stopped at the nearest bottle shop and bought a slab of beer and again at the store where he usually bought his imported cigarettes. He drove home, carefully minding the speed limits.

Chapter 11

He didn't have to feign outrage at the invasion of his house but then he had to act like a concerned relative.

"I was coming to talk to Constable Dwyer," Inspector Kent told Edward Dwyer. "He was here when I spoke to him on the phone. He seems to have disappeared. I wonder if you would care to tell me where you've been."

"Out to get some beer and smokes," Eddy Dwyer claimed, knowing the proof would be visible to the sticky-nosed cops. "Ted was still asleep when I left and Hilda, my wife, went out earlier to get a new dress. It's our anniversary at the end of the week and I promised to take her out."

Kent nodded. The patrol officer who was now near Dwyer's car had nodded that the words seemed true.

"I was here to ask your nephew, Constable Dwyer, about a claim made by his brother and sister that a packet of money, counterfeit they say, was in the house. Would you know anything about that?"

"I only got back off the boat last night, and those two weren't talking to me this morning. I can only guess it was because they were planning this mischief. If there is such a packet in my house, I know nothing about it. I know that Tom had a packet of money in his locker. The school told Ted about it – I assume you were also told of it?"

Kent nodded, cautiously.

"Look, I know you need to check out the story, so if you want to look around, please do. I'm afraid that my niece and nephew have probably been lying to you, trying to annoy me and inconvenience you."

Dwyer pursed his lips as if he was deciding whether to talk of something unpleasant.

"Ted tries his best with Tom and Jo, but the fact of the matter is that they are wild and unruly brats. I know they were well behaved when they stayed with you, no doubt to impress you, they are devious enough, but they are argumentative, always lying to me, they have to be forced to do their share of the work around here, ..."

Dwyer went on itemising Tom and Jo's faults, repeating what he had told the teacher at their school.

"I think you put the fear of God into them when you questioned them," Dwyer continued blithely. "I think that's why they went and pinched some gin from me. Somehow they got the cupboard open – I usually have it locked."

"I'll have another word with them," Kent said briskly, not implying that he thought Dwyer was lying himself. "With your permission, I will have a look around inside. There might be an indication of where Constable Dwyer went."

Dwyer led the way inside again; sure the police had already looked around. He led the policeman upstairs to check Ted's room, which looked as if he had just risen from sleep and the wet towel in the laundry suggested that he had just had a shower. Tom and Jo's rooms looked in order as did the kitchen and lounge room downstairs.

Dwyer unlocked his den and allowed the policeman to enter first.

Kent saw the mess in the room. "Looks like someone searched in here."

Dwyer pushed in past the policeman and scowled.

"This is Tom and Jo's idea of fun," he said coldly. "Keep this door locked, but they still seem to get in. They no doubt did it to spite me."

Kent lifted a rug off the floor and put it back on the couch. It felt damp in the spot he touched. Under it was a roll of sticky tape and some scissors. He turned around slowly, scanning the room, nothing struck him as suspicious but he decided if Dwyer were being so cooperative, there would be nothing to find. He would still like to do a thorough search in here, but he had no grounds for that. There was a dolphin torch on the floor by the couch and Kent picked it up casually, flicked it on, and off to see if it worked. He lifted it and twisted it, seeing then what might be blood in the groove when the lens cover screwed on.

"There's blood on the torch," Kent stated, watching for a reaction from Dwyer. The man was startled. "I'll have to take this for analysis. I think it will also be necessary to test the room for prints. It is beginning to look like Constable Dwyer surprised an intruder, and perhaps went off after him."

Kent seemed not to notice Dwyer's sudden agitation.

"Could I use your phone please?"

Dwyer nodded.

"Please don't touch anything."

"No, I won't. I don't know what anyone could want in here."

"Do you keep anything valuable in here? Money or electronic stuff?"

"No, nothing like that. Though who knows what Tom or Jo might come in here after."

"Well, they couldn't have done anything in here today. If you were around when they got up, and I personally saw them to school. I will be told if they step out of line there."

Kent was aware that Dwyer was listening to his call so he simply requested a lab team. The rest of his report could wait until he was in his car. Then he thought of Ted's car, still parked out in the street. He hadn't gone off in that. So where was he?

One o'clock came, and Constable Dwyer had not reported for work. He would have if he were able to, would have phoned if he could not. Dwyer was always punctual.

The lab report on the torch had not come through yet – Kent was sure that the blood would match Constable Dwyer's. The fingerprint team had sent a preliminary report, lots of Edward Dwyer's prints, and he had no record, and many unidentified prints. Some of the latter may prove to match the prints of the rest of the family; they were told to take prints from the bedrooms for comparison. A few prints had been matched to known thieves.

As a precaution, Kent had requested all police units too look out for Constable Dwyer.

Kent stood up suddenly, and grabbed his coat. He should speak to Tom and Jo before they heard any rumours. His phone rang; it was his superior, asking if any word had come in about the missing Constable. He had to report a lack of news, and request that the media be asked to tell the public to look out for the missing man. However, he told his superior to wait until he had spoken to Dwyer's brother and sister.

Half way to the school, he had a phone call patched through to his car radio.

"Dad, its Wendy. Jo and Tom are missing — we can't find them anywhere."

"I'm on my way, Wendy. Talk to you soon."

Kent sped up but did not use his siren. As he pulled into the school, he heard on the radio a news broadcast and mention was made of the missing policeman. He immediately called the radio room and asked to speak to the assistant commissioner. Nothing had been released officially — he would check.

Kent did not wait for the reply; he went striding to the administration block at a fast walk. Both William and Wendy were pacing around the front office, waiting for him. They told him quickly what had happened and that Hendry had all the year twelve students checking the school buildings and grounds for Tom and Jo Dwyer.

"You were meant to stay with her," Wendy was reminded.

"No, Dad, You told her to stay with me!" Wendy argued. "She said she needed to go to the toilet. I went with her. She somehow climbed out a window. I didn't realise until things had been quiet for a few minutes and she didn't answer when I said something to her."

Tom had done the same.

"Do you have any idea why?" Kent asked his children.

"No," Wendy was almost in tears. "Jo was acting odd at the end of lunch. I thought she was planning something but she promised it wasn't any tricks. When they both disappeared, we told the teacher and were sent up here to tell Hendry. Dad, what's wrong?"

"Is there any chance that Tom or Jo could have heard a news bulletin during lunch?"

Wendy nodded. "Some of the girls listen to their own radios during lunch — why?"

"Ted Dwyer is missing," Kent told his children. "Somehow the press got hold of it. He wasn't at his house when I went back this morning and he hasn't reported for work or called in."

"Dad," Will spoke up. "Tom thinks the sun shines out of his brother. If they heard he was missing, they probably went looking for him."

"Where would they look? Home?" Kent asked

"No, they wouldn't go there if their brother wasn't there," Wendy said with certainty.

"Because they don't like their uncle?"

"Yeah, pretty much," Will agreed without going into detail.

"I will put a call out for all units to look for those two little fools." Kent decided.

"Dad, there is one thing," Wendy interrupted. "I told Jo that I thought the woman we saw with their uncle that time was the one that worked at the dress shop mum used to go to."

Kent had an unreadable expression.

"When you find them, you won't send them home will you?" Wendy asked fearfully.

"I know what I'd like to do with them, but no, I'll make other arrangements," Kent betrayed his concern. "What time did they go off and how long was it before the students went looking for them?"

"Just after the lunch break, about a quarter to two," Will admitted. "It was about half an hour later before they started checking around the school."

"Ok, leave this with me," Kent told his children. "Call me if they turn up. I'll have a word with Hendry."

Kent strode to the Deputy Principal's office.

"You didn't tell him that Jo had your mobile phone," Will remarked to his twin.

"I wish I'd known what she wanted with it," Wendy replied. "Even if we'd known what they were planning I'd have let her have it, but I wish they'd told us. Even if we couldn't have stopped them, we could have warned Dad."

"Would she have it on?" Will suggested.

Wendy shook her head. "I doubt it. She has no way to recharge the battery. I hope she'll use it if they need help!"

Kent returned, trailed by Hendry.

"When you go back to class, pick up Tom and Jo's stuff and bring it here at the end of the lesson," Hendry directed the two worried students. "Then you'd better stay with your class."

Will nodded, preferring to help search, but obedient to orders.

Chapter 12

Running off wasn't completely without thought. Jo had heard the news about Ted on the radio and told Tom in a brief moment when neither Will nor Wendy were close enough to overhear. Both had absconded from school in the past and knew how to avoid being seen, but this time needed a bit more thought. They were certain that if they went off this time, the police would be looking for them too, and their blue school uniforms would be a handicap. They would be spotted too readily.

Jo had suggested looking for old clothes. The wardrobe in the corridor outside the drama room had a large selection, was never locked and wasn't far from the toilets. Tom knew how his sister was thinking and agreed. Slipping out from the toilets was easy, he knew from past experience.

Tom met Jo outside the drama room, which was in use at the time, but no one questioned their presence at the cupboard. They chose suitable items and bundled them into as small a size as possible, then walked quickly to the end of the corridor and left the building. They were facing the back of the school and it was only a short distance from the back gate.

Once out the gate, they ran as fast as they could until just before the shops near their home. They used the service station toilets to change out of their highly noticeable school uniform. Now, from a distance, they would look like two boys.

They still felt exposed, walking along the main road with a bundle of their school uniform, so opted to take back roads to their immediate destination.

Tom knew the way to Mrs Daniels house. Ted had told them she would help them if they ever felt unsafe at home.

It did not worry either of them that Mrs Daniel's car was not in the drive when they arrived. They just crept around the back, found a secluded corner of her garden, and waited. Now the rush from school was over, they had a chance to plan their next actions.

"Do you remember the way to those shops?" Jo asked Tom. "Wendy said the dress shop was in that group of shops where we saw uncle."

"I know the way," Tom assured her. "I'd still like to know what uncle was doing there if he was meant to be on a boat – and where he was staying. Do you think he's having an affair with that woman?"

"It's the only idea I could think of," Jo said. "If we can find her address and watch her place…"

"Uncle may not go there for days…" Tom interrupted. "And what if people notice us hanging around?"

"It will be evening or night, mostly," Jo told him. "If we don't see uncle, we may be able to peek in through the windows during the day."

"I can't see any other option," Tom agreed, not having to tell Jo how dangerous their plan was. "We are going to need some money though."

"When Mrs D. comes home we can ask her to lend us some," Jo proposed.

However, later that evening, Kath Daniels still was not home. Tom and Jo were forced to move to her back veranda for cover when a thunderstorm passed over. By morning, they were tired, cold and hungry.

Ted Dwyer vaguely remembered periods of wakefulness – when all he could feel was the ache of his muscles, the inability to move, the difficulty in drawing a breath and a thirst so acute it was a torment to endure.

The darkness, he gradually realised, was a hood of some kind over his head. It smelt musty, and as he tried to open his eyes, he felt something sticky catching his eyelids. The same stuff was around his mouth.

There was no sound except for his own breathing, and he had to fight panic and keep his breathing even. He began to remember going into his uncle's den. He remembered a packet, a heavy packet, too heavy to be money. Then the pain of the blow to his head. If he moved at all, his head throbbed, so he tried not to move. Was he still at the house?

Kent was on his way back to the house. Could he expect rescue soon? Had Uncle Ed returned? Who had hit him – his Uncle? Did his uncle know he was under suspicion? Was that why he had taken off so fast earlier. Had he meant to take that package away?

Did uncle care if he was tied up? Ted groaned, and something kicked him in the side.

"Still alive, Boss," a voice said close by. "Nah, no one will find him here."

Ted realised that the man was talking on a mobile phone. The realisation came that he was not still in his uncle's den. His uncle must have returned, and known he'd seen the package and taken him somewhere – was he planning to kill him? Did his uncle know that Tom and Jo had seen money in his den? What would happen to Tom and Jo when they came home from school? Did Kent know he was missing? Surely, he'd know and have people looking for him. Would he get Tom and Jo from school and keep them safe?

He had told Kent about his fears for them. Surely, he would.

Tom and Jo walked to the shops near Henty Park. They left soon after the sun rose and stopped only once at a service station, to get a hotdog and coke. Jo had only had a few dollars on her at school and that was almost gone now.

One thing about walking, it warmed them up. They maintained a steady pace and reached the shops about an hour before they were due to open. They found the dress shop easily enough, and a place out front where they could watch it. Then, because they didn't want to be noticed hanging around, they walked around the block of shops and found a laneway that led behind the dress shop. They decided to investigate this and had some luck. The shop that backed onto the dress shop had a small back courtyard containing a pile of boxes.

"If we rearrange these, one of us could hide here and watch the back," Jo mused. "Both of us could wait here until the shop opens."

They made a quick job of making a hidey-hole.

"Will you go in when they open," Tom asked Jo.

"I don't know," Jo told him. "I don't exactly look like I have money to spend and I look more like a boy. I'll go in if there is no other choice."

They heard voices approaching and fell silent.

The day was a frustrating waste of time. Tom and Jo split up and spent alternating periods at the front and back of the dress shop. The only breaks they took were to visit the toilet and get water from the taps there to slake their thirst. At those times, the one out of position would report to the other.

When it drew near to five o'clock, Jo removed her cap, let her hair out and slipped into the shop with a small group of girls her age.

The other girls were making enough noise to keep the shop woman's eye on them. Jo tried to remain inconspicuous as she looked at the racks at the back of the shop, near the woman's office space. She glanced at the woman, and when she seemed busy with the other girls, Jo slipped into the little back room and looked around. She had no idea how to find where the woman lived, and went first to the little table that seemed to serve as a desk. Nothing there looked promising. There was a filing cabinet that was locked, and boxes of papers.

Jo turned to leave the room and saw, hanging on a hook just inside the door, a bunch of keys.

"Stupid woman!" Jo muttered to herself, as she reached for them. They keys had an address tag on them, giving her what she needed without having to try and find the key to open the filing cabinet. As soon as she had memorised the address, Jo put the keys back and ducked out of the office. She was looking at jeans when the woman approached her and politely told her the shop was closing. Jo smiled and shrugged before turning to leave the shop.

"The woman is an idiot," Jo told her brother, filling him in on what she had found.

"Uncle likes stupid women!" Tom commented when Jo had finished.

Jo shrugged, not wanting to think about him. "How do we find out where this Willow Street is?"

"Reckon Will or Wendy will know?" Tom proposed.

"I don't want to get them in trouble. Even though their father has been nice to us, I doubt he will be impressed with us nicking off. He'd be very annoyed if he thought Wendy or Will helped us," Jo decided. "I'd hate to think what he'd say to us."

"I'd say that 'nice' wouldn't describe it," Tom told her.

"Do you think we should back off and let the police look for Ted?"

"No!" was Tom's definite reply.

"All right, I'll call Will and pretend to be Julie if Aunt Gayle answers. Wendy reckons he likes Julie."

Jo still had enough coins for the public phone, hoping they would not need to talk for long.

They decided it was better than using Wendy's mobile phone, if for instance her father answered and recognised the number on his phone display.

Jo was relieved when Wendy answered.

"Wendy? It's Jo."

"Jo, where are you? Dad's really worried about you."

"Wen, please don't tell him we called. We just need to know how to get from the shops we went to that time, to Willow Street, South Melbourne," Jo pleaded.

"I'll get the street directory, talk to Will for a minute."

"Jo, you little idiot, Dad's livid, where are you?"

"Will, we're looking for Ted. We've found where the woman lives."

"So has Dad. He's out there at the moment. Let him handle things!"

"No, we'll try to keep in touch. If you find out what he knows, could you tell us?"

"He usually doesn't discuss his work with us, but I'll try. Oh, your uncle is still at your place acting concerned relative."

"It had to be him," Jo accused. "That's why we don't think the police will find anything. He's too careful – but he won't expect trouble from us."

"Jo, don't be an idiot. Come back here!"

"No, we're going to find Ted."

Wendy returned and took the phone from her brother.

"Jo? Do you have a pen and paper?"

"Just tell me."

Wendy gave directions to Willow Street and added. "It's a good five miles."

"Thanks Wen, we'll keep in touch."

Jo hung up.

Chapter 13

Willow Street was partly back towards their own house, but further west. Tom and Jo set off with determination. They were feeling the evening chill, but hoped walking would keep them warm and their minds off their hunger. They kept on, ignoring their aching feet, only slowing a bit to ease the discomfort.

It was full dark when they reached Willow Street, and they felt safe enough walking along it to get a glimpse of the house at number 27. In the dark, it looked tidy enough, but the neighbourhood was not much different to their own.

They kept walking, so as not to betray their interest in the house. Several cars were parked nearby; one had two dark figures in it.

"Stake out," Tom muttered knowingly.

"Good!" Jo commented. "What do we do now – we can't creep around the house if it is being watched."

"Keep walking. I think there might be a shop up ahead. Do you have enough money for a can of drink?"

"That will be about all!"

There was a group of youths hanging around outside the shop, most looked to be older than eighteen. All of them eyed, the two strangers without greeting them.

Tom followed Jo into the shop and they bought one can of coke and decided to sit outside and share it. By moving his chair a little, Tom could look down the street towards number 27.

After a while, the tallest of the loitering youths strolled across to their table.

"Good evening," Jo said politely non-committal.

"What would two babies be doing out this late at night," was the return greeting. It was spoken in an insulting drawl.

Tom glanced at the speaker, not rising to the insult.

"We aren't planning to give you any trouble, if that's what you are worried about."

Tom returned to staring down the street.

"Who are you planning trouble for?" the youth asked, following the direction of Tom's gaze.

"Nobody you would want to know!" Jo said sourly, turning away.

The tall youth dragged another chair over and sat astride of it, facing the strangers over the chair's back.

"Any trouble that happens around here, I want to know about!" he snarled. "Because, when there's trouble around here, it's me and my mates that get questioned."

"Then you'd better run off home and hide!" Tom suggested politely calm. "There are two men in a car back there down the street."

At a nod from the tall youth, one of the other boys casually dropped his skateboard to the ground and scooted off.

"The police were there earlier," was the thoughtful reply. "At the house of the dress shop dame. Is that who you are after?"

"No," Jo took a turn to answer. "It's a family matter. We are trying to find our older brother."

"Do you think he's shacking up with her?" The youth was almost laughing but he quickly turned serious. "You better hope he isn't. Or if he is, that he's not there when her old man is. Right bastard he is."

"Are they married?" Tom asked pointedly.

"Huh, doubt it. Who'd want that old broad? He just lives there when he's not travelling for his business."

"What does he do?" Jo decided to ask. She saw the tall youth's eyes grow shrewd.

"Is he living there now?" Tom added quickly.

"Not sure. I didn't see him last night. I think he was around the night before that. He might have gone off again."

Tom glanced at Jo. The exchange was observed by the other youth.

"If you two kids have stuff to sell – don't go to him. Go somewhere else."

The warning was meant sincerely, whatever it was about.

"Is the bloke…?" Jo carefully described her uncle as they had seen him near the shops, not in the sloppy clothes he wore at home.

"Could be…"

"Do you know his name?" Tom asked urgently.

"Yeah, Dawson. Eddy Dawson."

"And where he works?" Tom asked again.

"It was her turn to ask!" the youth pointed at Jo. He seemed to be considering his answer.

"Who does he work for?" Jo asked with a faint grin.

"What do I get out of this if I help you?"

The youth was eying Jo.

"We haven't got anything to offer," Tom admitted slumping back in his chair.

Jo turned her eyes away as she sensed the youth's meaning. "Not even myself," she said with a visible shudder.

The boy with the skateboard returned. "Cops, right enough," he reported.

"He probably won't come here," Tom said to Jo. "She'll have warned him."

"No, Aunt Hilda can't contact him when he's away. I doubt he'd give her any way to contact him either," Jo argued. "He might…"

"Unless they are watching him at home and he knows it. He won't move," Tom countered.

"It's the only clue we've got," Jo insisted. "I say we hang around until morning until she's gone to work. If the stake out is gone, we look around."

"Hey!"

Tom and Jo both looked at the taller boy.

"I don't know what you two think you are going to do – but you're idiots! Even I can see you're still wet behind the ears. You'll be caught before you can blink. If you are lucky – it will be the police. You don't want to fall foul of Dawson. I'll bet you've never even spent a night on the streets before."

"We have!" Tom stated, thinking of the previous night.

"And we'll keep doing it until we find our brother," Jo added, eyes flashing with determination. "The police have too many rules to follow. We don't follow rules. And I won't go back home unless Ted is there!"

Again, the shudder was more eloquent than words.

The tall youth stood up and went to speak a few quiet words to his mates. All but one melted away into the night.

"Come with me!" the tall youth ordered, looking back at Tom and Jo. Their expression clearly asked, "Why?"

"We can't talk here, and Jack will get you something to eat."

The mention of food did the trick. Tom and Jo decided to follow the other two boys who led them through a narrow gap between the fence and the corner of the shop. It led to a narrow paved way that continued to the back of the shop where the owners had their living quarters. They didn't go in there, instead they all climber a narrow metal staircase to the floor above the shop. The boy, Jack, unlocked the door and entered first.

Inside there was a bed, table, two chairs and numerous beanbags. The tall youth closed the door behind every one and collapsed into a pile of three beanbags.

"I'm Rick," he said, waving Tom and Jo to sit down. They did so more cautiously.

"I'm Tom," Tom offered.

"Jo."

"If I understand your conversation," Rick began, "You think that bastard Dawson is your uncle?"

"Could be…" Tom imitated Rick's earlier comment.

"Bastard is an apt description," Jo agreed.

"Why exactly are you trying to find him?"

"We don't want to find him. We want to find our brother, Ted. Uncle is probably at home right now, smirking into his beer. But we are sure he's involved in taking Ted away and it's probably our fault." Tom did not like admitting that point.

Between them, Tom and Jo told Rick of the odd phone call, finding the package, telling the Inspector of it and becoming aware that the police were starting to take an interest in their uncle. They then told how they had heard their brother was missing and how they believed their uncle must have caught him when he was checking out their claim.

"So your brother is a policeman and this Inspector is…"

"A family friend, but even though we're friends with his kids he didn't let us off easy when we were in trouble at school."

"For what it's worth, you've got my help," Rick said finally. "Jack, go and get some grub will ya."

Rick stayed quiet until Jack's footsteps had faded down the steps.

"Dawson shopped me once," Rick told them. "Now I try to stay clear of him. But, I'd really like to be able to put a boot in his face."

"Shopped you? Put the police on you?" Jo queried. Rick nodded, savagely. "And he lied a damn torrent so I was sent up for two years. All I'd done was nick a couple of watches. I heard he was the best receiver for such stuff, so I went to him. Do you know what he did? While he was talking to me, he had his mate call the cops and when they arrived, he claimed that I had been trying to make him buy not just the watches but some other jewellery as well. They believed him, not me. He was the honest citizen. I was the boob who was his means of getting rid of some stuff too hot to sell. I heard he even claimed the reward for finding some of the stuff."

"Our uncle acts nice to Ted and our teachers, but he's a bastard to us. If Dawson isn't uncle, he's the same type," Jo commented.

"Well, I don't know that your brother would be at his digs. It would mean he'd have to trust a woman, but he has a warehouse - Dawson Imports, in Greyson Street. I can take you there."

"How far is it?" Tom asked, reminded of his aching feet. He was as tired as if he had been doing sport all day.

"Not far. I can get us a lift for most of the way, but we'd best walk the last bit."

"That'll do," Jo agreed. "Then we'll find a way in."

They all heard footsteps returning up the metal stairs. Jack reappeared with two microwave-heated pizzas and four cans of coke.

"Dig in," Rick invited. His guests didn't need a second invitation.

"We're going for Dawson's warehouse," Rick told Jack.

"Count me in," Jack said.

"No, Jack. If he turned up, you'd be in strife. He knows you by sight."

"He knows you too," Jack protested.

"He hasn't seen me close up for over two years," Rick countered. "Besides, I want to know what goes on down the street. You live here – gives you a good reason to be hanging around."

"You just going with them," Jack pointed.

Rick shook his head.

"I was going to ask Spark to lend us his car and Mitch to tag along."

"We don't want to get you in more trouble," Tom said when he'd swallowed his mouthful of pizza.

"We'll be careful," Rick promised. He had no desire to go back to the detention centre. However, he was eighteen now. If he was caught out, it would be jail this time.

He turned to Tom and Jo.

"Spark is good with electricity. His old man is a linesman, taught him a lot. He wants Spark to be one too, or an electrician. I met Mitch when I was away. He's gifted at opening things."

Rick saw the eyes of the two teenagers begin to glisten with anticipation.

"Rick, we appreciate your help," Tom said, and he meant it. "We promise that we won't mention you or your friends to the police. If we get caught in the warehouse, we'll say we snuck in."

"There may be nothing there," Rick warned. "Dawson only keeps a small amount of imported stuff around. He keeps what he receives somewhere else. I don't know where, but we might find a clue."

"We have to check. Ted's been missing for almost two days now," Jo insisted.

Rick didn't suggest to his new friends that their brother might not even be still alive.

"Don't walk so fast!" Rick warned, slowing his companions who seemed to have recovered some of their energy.

"Why?"

Tom was frustrated keeping to a slouching amble.

"The cops patrol around here frequently. If they see you walking fast, they think you've nicked something and they will hassle you. Or they'll think you've been vandalising something."

Tom slowed, not wanting that sort of attention. He was sure that Kent would have the police looking for them.

Two blocks further on, Rick led them down a laneway, crossed another street and continued along another lane. This ended near a railway line, where there was only a wire fence between them and the tracks. They walked single file along the narrow space until they spotted two figures up ahead.

Rick whistled softly and the two figures stopped what they were doing and began to approach. Both figures seemed to slip something into their pockets as they walked.

"Rick," one greeted.

"Who are these," the other asked.

"A couple of kids who want to kick Eddy Dawson where it hurts."

"How?" the first one asked.

"We want to get into his warehouse and see if he's keeping our brother there," Tom spoke for himself. "Or find a clue if he's not."

"He's paranoid about security," the second boy said flatly.

"Would he rush over if his alarms went off?" Jo asked thoughtfully.

"If not him, one of his mates," was the general agreement.

"Can we borrow your car, Spark?" Rick asked. "We won't be taking it too close."

"Done! I'll have a quick word with my dad. He may know how to get the power off to the alarm."

"Won't he want to know why?" was Tom's concern.

"If I tell him we're out to get Dawson, he'll want to help!" Spark reassured Tom. "And if I tell him you're looking for your brother…"

"Who is a policeman," Jo decided to add.

"He won't talk." Spark assured her.

Chapter 14

Jo crouched down next to her brother in a patch of shadow between two buildings. They were not far from Dawson's warehouse. Rick, their new friend, stood back further - watching the street. Mitch and Spark had gone off with Hal, Sparks' father.

"Should we be doing this," Jo asked nervously.

"No, but when has that stopped us. This is for Ted!" Tom whispered back. He was nervous too.

"We should call the Inspector," Jo suggested.

"What can he do? He has to have a good reason to go in there," Tom said. "When we've got a good reason for him, you can call him on Wendy's phone."

"Psst."

Spark ran into the shadow. "The door is open and the power is off. Alarms should be too. Here's a torch. If the lights go on – get out!"

Tom sprinted across the deserted road. Jo was only a pace behind him. There kept together as they entered through a small door that was indeed unlocked, next to a roller door. Tom gave silent thanks to their new friends.

The torch seemed very bright and gave them plenty of light so they could avoid the pallets and crates on the floor. They peeped into the smaller cubicles, three of them, all of which were unlocked and completely empty. Tom crept upstairs to another cubicle that proved to be a sparsely furnished office. It had a table two chairs and a filing cabinet. Tom tried the cabinet, it too was unlocked, and it contained neat folders of order and delivery dockets. The writing on everything was in their uncle's handwriting. Tom looked no further and returned to where Jo waited on the warehouse floor.

"Nothing. It's too neat and nothing is locked. He can't have anything incriminating here."

"Mitch said he was paranoid about security," Jo reminded her brother. "You know what he's like at home. What is here? Nothing that needs to be hidden. Now I don't think our good fairies did more than open the door and turn of the power to the alarms…"

90

Tom thought about what Rick had said.

"If he meets thieves here – and there is no sign of stolen stuff – where does he take it and how? I can't see him walking with it outside. Though I suppose he could drive his car in here and load it up. We can't stay in here much longer."

"Look for sensors," Jo whispered suddenly.

Tom shone the torch around the warehouse, trying to avoid the windows. They saw movement sensors in the corners, dead now, without the power on. There were no other sensors – not on the windows, not on the walls and nothing around the pallets on the floor.

Suddenly a single down light came on.

"We've got to go," Jo urged, dragging on Tom's arm.

They began to sprint to the door when Tom stopped suddenly.

"I want to check those rooms again."

In the middle one, they found a sensor across the door.

They examined the floor this time and saw what looked like a rough hole in the patterned concrete. Tom knelt down and put his finger into it and part of the floor began to lift.

Jo watched as a tunnel was revealed. The trapdoor was made of wood covered by a thin layer of patterned cement.

"Tom, Jo. Hurry!" Rick called from the door. "The alarms will go back on in a sec and a guard is coming."

Tom stuck his head out the door of the cubicle.

"Go, Rick. We've found a tunnel. Set the alarm off. If the attention is here, it will cover us."

"Idiots!"

"Go on!"

Tom disappeared back into the room. "I'll go first," he told Jo. "You pull the door back down after you. If any of uncle's men arrive, we don't want them to think we found this."

Tom shone the torch down the hole. The first part was a four-foot drop, and then there were steps. He helped to lift Jo after she dropped so she could close the door.

They had to mind their heads for the first few steps, but after that they had plenty of headroom.

Rick watched the patrolling security guard draw closer. Mitch and Spark were still with Hal in the power service access tunnel. Mitch had gone to tell Hal of the guard so he could reconnect one part of the power to warn the kids.

The door to the warehouse was closed but not locked. Would the man actually check it? He was meant to, but what would he do then? Call Dawson or call the police?

Rick knew which option he'd prefer. The police had ethics, Dawson did not.

There! The guard had found the door unlocked, but what was he doing? Going in? Odd! The alarms didn't go off! Had Hal not returned the power to that circuit? Or had the guard turned it off?

The main lights went back on inside.

Rick remembered to breathe. Where were those kids? He expected any minute that the guard would find them. The guards normally didn't enter premises where thieves might be.

Rick felt in his pockets for anything he could use if he had to help the kids get free. All he had was a small coil of wire, a small shifter and screwdriver. He started to move, but just then, the lights went off across the road. The blinking red light below the alarm came back on and the guard reappeared, alone, and relocked the door. As he walked away, he drew out a mobile phone.

A soft whistle alerted Rick to Mitch's approach. "The kids are still inside," Rick told his friend.

"The alarms are on," Mitch confirmed.

"So where did they go? The guard can't have found them. He wasn't inside long enough. Tom said he found a tunnel. He was in one of the side offices."

"Must be where Dawson stashes stuff." Mitch decided. "Do you think it is a tunnel or just an underground room?"

"I'd bet on a tunnel," Rick said. "Rats like Dawson always have an escape hole."

"To the outside or another building?" Mitch asked. "What are you going to do?"

"Let's check out the nearest buildings. If all seem deserted, we wait. If someone else turns up, we set off the alarms in Dawson's. I'll start; you go warn Spark to move out."

Tom and Jo walked quietly along the tunnel. It had dull illumination so they turned off the torch. If it wasn't for the fact that they were together and the hope that their uncle was being watched by the police, neither would have dared to go this far. They were fully aware of the enormity of what they were doing. This was breaking and entering, not mischief and tricks.

Up ahead was a slightly brighter chamber. Tom and Jo slowed, but the only sound they heard was their own breathing. They entered the room and separately crept around the walls on opposite sides of the machinery in the centre. There were two doors on each side, all locked. At each, they knocked softly and listened at the door. At the other side of the room was a second set of stairs.

"There will be alarms upstairs," Tom whispered. "What do you want to do?"

"Pull these berets down and keep our faces down," Jo suggested. "And try to search really fast."

"Wait a mo'" Tom said as he began to examine the machinery. It looked like a printing press. He grabbed something from the shelf below it. It was a Stanley knife, and he closed it before pocketing it.

Without warning, a red light began to flash and a low buzzer sounded. The light was above the tunnel they had entered through.

"Let's hurry," Tom urged. There was a door closing across the far entrance and Tom didn't want to risk being caught in the secret chamber if another closed on this side.

The second tunnel was lit like the first and they travelled along it to the end, where a second trapdoor covered it. They raised the trapdoor slowly and were reassured by the dull security lighting. When they crept out, they didn't close the door after them this time.

They expected alarms to ring, but none did.

"Maybe," Jo whispered. "This must be their escape route if the other building is entered. The door would delay the police and give them time to get out here. So they don't have the alarms on here if they have to flee."

"Whatever!" Tom said with distraction. "There are rooms all around here."

These rooms were all padlocked, except for one. When they opened the door and shone their torch in, they saw an unmoving body.

Ignoring caution, they ran to the figure, relieved to hear breathing, harsh though it was.

Tom gently lifted the head as Jo removed the musty hood. The figure struggled weakly.

"Lie still, Ted!" Jo whispered. "Tom, can you cut the tape off his mouth?"

Tom adjusted the Stanley knife and worked carefully, whilst Jo drew out Wendy's phone, turned it on and input the code.

"I haven't got a signal in here," Jo nearly panicked.

"Move around," Tom advised, not stopping what he was doing. "Or see if you can find a normal phone."

Jo moved back out into the main part of the building, but still couldn't get a signal. She looked for an office and saw one in the same place as in the building next door. She ran to the stairs and began to climb. Finally, she had signal on the mobile. As she listened to the dial tone, she glanced down at the warehouse floor and saw two dark figures moving cautiously along the floor below, looking right and left. She dared not call out to Tom, and moved herself into the office.

"Kent!" Jo heard the phone answered. She had dialled the inspector's mobile number.

"It's Jo Dwyer. We've found Ted, but we need help."

"Where are you?"

Jo quickly described where they had come, the Dawson building, the tunnel and machinery and where they now were, as best she could.

Jo stopped talking to listen to Kent's instructions. Hearing a slight sound, she glanced up and saw a man aiming a gun at her.

"Well, well, well, Boss said there'd be two," a rough voice spoke. "Put the phone down!"

Jo gulped and carefully put the phone down without ending the call.

The man sidled over to the desk, keeping his gun aimed at her. The man removed his gaze from her for a moment to reach for the phone; making the mistake of thinking Jo was scared stiff.

Anger boiled up in Jo. She took that moment's lapse in concentration to spring down under the man's gun arm and drive her head into his groin. He dropped the phone as he bellowed and reached for the painful area. Jo grabbed the gun, then scooted for the door and slammed it before running down the steps. She made no attempt at silence; speed was her concern.

"Watch out, Jo!" she heard Tom scream at her.

The warning was timely, she saw a flash and heard a muffled report, and ducked in time for the bullet to pass over her head.

She heard sounds of a scuffle.

"Run Jo! Get out!"

"You little bastard," a familiar voice growled. Jo looked to the front of the warehouse where the roller door was, but decided against running to that door. There had to be a door at this end. Yes, there was, under the stairs.

Jo struggled with the heavy bar across the door, trying desperately to lift it as the stairs above her rang with the heavy tread of the man she'd hurt.

"Bitch!"

Jo was grabbed from behind and slammed into the wall. She stumbled back, still in the man's grip. Her face hurt and her ears buzzed. She couldn't hear what it was that caused the man to stop.

Tom had eased the tape on Ted's mouth and cut the tape around his wrists and ankles. He had no warning when he was grabbed from behind and pulled away from his brother. His beret was pulled off and his head was jerked around. Tom looked into a pair of eyes, blazing with hate.

"Where is your sister?" Eddy Dwyer/Dawson snarled.

"Outside," Tom lied. "Calling the police."

A moment later an enraged bellow echoed around the almost empty main warehouse chamber."

"Try again!"

"Watch out, Jo!" Tom yelled, before a beefy fist turned his face into agony. The hurried steps on the metal staircase alerted Dwyer and he threw Tom onto the concrete floor and looked out of the room's door. He fired one shot at a dark figure on the stairs.

Dwyer saw Spiv stumbling down the stairs and turned his attention back to Tom. The little bitch wouldn't be able to open the back door.

"You are an interfering brat," Dwyer snarled at Tom. "You've nosed into my business once too often."

Tom was vaguely aware of sirens getting louder, but his uncle seemed unconcerned.

"How'd you get in?"

"Snuck in," Tom claimed. "Door was open."

"I don't believe you!"

Tom felt his already sore face struck twice more as his uncle slapped him.

"Eddy! The trapdoor is up and the bitch was talking on a mobile phone."

Now Dwyer was alarmed. He took Tom in a fierce grip and dragged him to the back door.

"Bring the girl!" Dwyer snapped.

"What about the cop!"

"He'll keep! He never saw you. These two know too much. We'll bring them and have them as hostages."

Tom and Jo stumbled as they were relentlessly forced to run. Dwyer held Tom with one hand as the other unbarred the door. The sirens were much louder as Dwyer and Spiv and their two prisoners raced between buildings to where Spiv's car was parked.

First Tom and then Jo tripped on the kerb of the road, slowing their captors.

"Hey! You! Stop, Security!" A voice yelled from nearby.

"I'm not finished with you!" Dwyer told Tom as he dropped him onto the road.

Spiv dropped Jo and the two men sprinted faster, quickly diving between two more buildings.

Rick and Mitch reached the two fallen figures, who were even then trying to stand up. Mitch continued on after the two men.

"Are you Ok?" Rick asked the teenagers who both had blood all over their faces.

Tom ignored the question.

"Ted's in there!" he pointed to the building they'd left.

"Help us back there!" Jo insisted, in spite of the blood and tears blinding her.

"The police are here! Let them handle it," Rick urged. "Do you want them to know you are here?"

"I called them," Jo told him. "We saw things we want them to know about. I don't care what happens then, if Ted's ok and uncle is caught."

"You don't haff to say," Tom told Rick. "You done - nuff."

"I'll help you back," Rick said flatly.

Mitch trotted back.

"They had a car — got away."

Mitch helped Jo to stand and hobble back, as Rick helped Tom.

Chapter 15

Inspector Kent wasted no time mobilising all available units to surround the area where Greyson Street was located. When he called the control room, he learnt that two units were already responding to an alarm call at the Dawson's Imports warehouse.

He didn't stop to wonder how the kids had found the place – when his staff hadn't known of it. It wasn't listed in any of the business or phone directories.

Kent used his siren to hurry to the scene, continuing to direct units as he drove. He was in turn advised that an ambulance was enroute.

The guard waited outside Dawson's. The first two units had already arrived. One officer was with the guard, the other three were inside. The alarms were still ringing loudly.

"I found it open on my earlier round," the man was saying. "So I locked the door and reported it. Fifteen minutes later, the alarm went off so I hurried back and waited for the police."

Kent had caught the end of the report as he walked over, and the three officers were re-emerging from the building. They recognised the Inspector.

"There is no one inside, Sir."

Kent looked around, considering what Jo Dwyer had said.

"I had a snitch that Constable Dwyer was here. There is a way from inside this building to another. Two of you come with me. I have other units coming. When they get here, I want these immediate buildings surrounded.

Kent led the way back inside. He found the control box for the alarm but couldn't silence it. It had a keypad control and needed a security number to silence it. He ignored the strident noise.

One of the patrol officers received a message via radio.

"Sir, the suspect you asked about is not at home."

Kent's feeling of alarm increased. He scanned the warehouse and walked to the centre of the three small side rooms.

"In here," he directed and led the way into the room. The floor here was patterned, not smooth.

He knelt down and fingered the gaps between several tiles. On the third try, he felt something move and lifted the trap door.

"Constable, get a torch, quickly."

The officer ran out to his car, searched under the seat for a moment and returned at a run.

Kent led the way down the stairway, that turned several times, and along the dimly lit tunnel. He was sure now which way the tunnel led. He was stopped at a solid metal door. He examined it briefly, and then directed his subordinates back upstairs.

"Find out who owns the building next to this," Kent pointed to the one separated by a wide laneway. See if we can get permission to go in. Constable, we'll see if there are any other entrances.

The four figures heading towards them looked like street kids that had been in a fight. Whatever, they didn't belong around here anyway.

One was bareheaded and blond, in the light from the street lamp. Kent took off at a run towards them.

"Tom? Jo?"

"Yes," Jo answered. "Ted's in there." She pointed shakily. "We'll be okay."

Kent looked at the building and saw the open door.

"Call for back up. Find out where the ambulance is. Get these kids to my car and keep them there."

Four more officers ran into view and followed Kent into the second building. They spread out to search.

Ted Dwyer was unconscious, but Kent saw that some of his bonds had been cut. Not the tape on the eyes though and only partly off the mouth.

Tom limped into the building, supported by Rick. He knelt by his brother, waiting for the ambulance to come. He watched in silence as the paramedics lifted the stretcher.

Kent studied the teenager.

"Good work," he said quietly.

"Youff got to get our uncle. He did this. Him and his mate."

"You are sure it's your uncle?"

Tom nodded.

"He's Dawson too. Next door. His writing is on ev'rything."

"How did you find out?"

Rick answered.

"I knew Dawson. Told him and his sister where this place was. Warned him that Dawson was dangerous."

"S'right, did – but we had to find Ted. Did you find the tunnel?"

"It was blocked."

"Not from this end."

"Sir, we found the other end of the tunnel," a constable reported.

"Print press," Tom added.

"See this boy gets medical attention and get his sister. I need to talk to them both. I want words with you too…"

"I'm Rick, Sir."

Kent nodded and strode off after the other officer.

"Jo's outside," Rick told the constable.

Mitch sidled up to Rick.

"Hal and Spark will wait another ten minutes then leave."

"You go, I'll stay," Rick told his friend. "Thanks for coming."

None of the police noticed Mitch go.

The officers concentrated on the two injured teenagers. Rick ambled after them and leant against the unmarked police car where they were taken. An ambulance officer began to do first aid on their facial injuries.

It was half an hour before Kent returned to his car. Jo was dozing on her brother's shoulder and Tom was almost asleep. It had been a long day.

Kent was surprised to find Rick still with Tom and Jo. He had expected the street kid to go as soon as he had a chance.

"Okay, what have you to do with all this mess," Kent asked Rick. "How do you know these two miscreants?"

Rick smiled faintly. "I only met them tonight and when they said they were after Eddy Dawson, I told them where this place was. Like I said, I tried to warn them off."

"And I suppose these two went haring off anyway?" Kent suggested.

"They thought he was their uncle and they were trying to find their brother."

Kent sighed in exasperation. "What do you know about Dawson?"

Rick glanced around nervously. "A few things," he admitted."

"Hop in," Kent ordered, as he went around to his driver's seat.

Rick settled uneasily in the passenger seat.

"What can you tell me," Kent encouraged.

Rick took a deep breath and repeated what he had told Tom and Jo.

Kent could understand the young man's initial reticence. He also sensed something decent about him.

"Do you know anything about the place next door?"

"Nothing, except that those two ended up in there. I didn't know they were connected. But the kid mentioned a tunnel. It makes sense. It would be how Dawson moved the hot stuff away so fast."

"Where can I find you if I need you?" Kent asked.

"I was staying at the Willow Street milk bar with Jack, but I don't think I'll go back there. Too close to Dawson's pad."

Kent spotted his superior climbing from a car not too far away.

"Wait here will you, I might need to get a statement from you."

Rick nodded and slumped down in the seat. If the two kids could risk so much to hurt Dawson, could he do less?

Kent stepped out and strode over to report to his superior.

"A good night's work, Kent," Chief Inspector Watts commented. "Show me what you found."

"Yes, Sir. I think we need a search warrant for the building where Dwyer was found."

"Oh, the door was open, evidence of a crime within?" Watts summarised.

"True, Sir, but I have reason to believe that the locked storage rooms may contain stolen goods."

"Explain?"

Kent mentioned what he had heard from Rick.

"Sour grapes! Dawson turned him in," Watts dismissed the report.

"If it wasn't for the fact of the tunnel, I'd agree with you," Kent disagreed. "Then there is the press. There is no sign of any plates to print from, but the ink stains are reddish – the colour for twenties. Nor did we see any printing paper, inks, etc. We'd need to search for those things."

"That much is logical," Watts agreed thoughtfully. "I'll organise the legal aspects. What is being done here?"

"I've got the area sealed off. The forgery team are examining the press set-up. Ted Dwyer is on his way to hospital. I have his sister and brother in my car – a little worse for wear. I have a call out for Dwyer's uncle. He slipped out on the watchers at his house, and it is almost certain that Eddy Dwyer and Eddy Dawson are the same man. Young Tom Dwyer saw him here."

"Dwyer's brother and sister are here?" Watts was startled. "Where do they come into this?"

"They found out where Dawson lived – were convinced, in spite of evidence to the contrary, that Dawson was their uncle – and found someone who knew of this place."

"Why didn't we get here sooner?" Watts wanted to know.

"We wouldn't have had enough evidence to search – and the Dawson building is clean except for the tunnel," Kent reminded him. "Jo Dwyer called me when they found their brother and told me of the tunnel."

"How did they get in," Watts demanded.

"I haven't asked them yet, Sir," Kent admitted. "They have proved to be resourceful and determined. I do not think they could have broken in without setting an alarm off. And if they had, they would need a code number to turn the alarm off. I would guess they snuck in before the place closed, or when the place was not locked. The guard found the Dawson building unlocked on one of his rounds, locked it and reset the alarms. We had a call a bit later when the alarm went off – but we found no one inside."

Kent decided not to mention the presence of an ex-con 'friend' of Tom and Jo.

"I hope you impress upon those two children – the folly of their actions," Watts insisted.

"Though, I am relieved that Constable Dwyer was found. I want a report of tonight's events on my desk tomorrow, including a statement from Dwyer's siblings. Arrange a guard for Constable Dwyer and the young ones. Their uncle! I wonder how long Edward Dwyer has been in this business – right under our noses."

"I don't know that," Kent said. "Edward Dwyer can act very civilised and polite when he wants to. He was always like that when Ted was around, but his siblings saw a different side. Ted was convinced they were merely being teenagers and resenting grownups."

"Well, tell those kids to keep out of our business in future – and watch their step," Watts snapped. "Where is this press?"

"I'll take you there, Sir."

"Just point the way, I'll find it. You continue with what you were doing."

Chapter 16

Tom and Jo went back to school on the Thursday, driven there by a police driver and would be taken home by the same officer. Home, at the moment, was the house of Kath Daniels. She had returned from her trip away and had no hesitation in offering Tom and Jo a place to stay. She went to great lengths to make them feel welcome and even managed to raise a smile when she commented about the white tape across both their noses. It made them look more like twins than ever, she said.

When they needed a shoulder to hide their faces on, she was there to hug and reassure them.

Tom and Jo ignored the stares as they walked to their homeroom. They spoke curt greetings to their classmates and forced smiles for their closest friends.

Wendy and Julie formed an escort for Jo and Mike and Will did the same for Tom, fending off unwelcome questions. The Kent twins knew what Tom and Jo had been through, but only told Mike and Julie.

Devin Rhodes merely welcomed them back, with only a trace of irony in his voice. He recognised signs of stress in their all too quiet behaviour. In fact, their current manner worried him more than when he thought they were planning mischief. He spoke to them quietly before their first period.

"Mr Scott wants a few words with you before your first period."

"Fine," Tom said.

"Thank you," Jo said, as they continued out the door in the company of their friends.

Rhodes followed slowly, saw Tom and Jo break off from their friends at the library entrance and continue onto the student foyer in the Admin Building. He increased his steps, so that he was at the entrance to the staff room when they walked into the office of the Principal's secretary. There wasn't anything else he could do.

Tom and Jo were shown in to see Scott at once and invited to sit down.

"Well," Scott began. "Was your escapade worth it?"

He took in the bandages, bruises and scratches that were vivid on the otherwise pale skin.

"We found our brother!" Tom said flatly, daring a contradiction.

"And he was alive!" Jo added. "Much longer and …" Jo didn't wish to speak the rest of her thought.

"So can I be assured that neither of you will run off like that again?"

"No," Jo answered, clinging to her books like they were a security blanket.

"No, I can't be assured, or no, you won't run off?"

"We won't run off," Tom clarified. "Sir, you don't need to give us a lecture. We've already had it. Don't leave school except with our driver, keep away from the perimeter of the school, keep with our friends, stay away from Fred Jackson…"

"That does seem to cover things. I won't tolerate a repeat or Monday's exercise. You survived your escapade with relatively minor injuries – next time you might not be so lucky."

Tom simply stared back at Scott. If he hadn't been told about their uncle's threats – Tom wasn't going to tell him.

"You may go back to your class. Pick up a chit from my secretary on the way out."

Neither Tom nor Jo felt like talking. Tom kicked at the chair outside the door as he passed. Scott wisely made no comment.

They rejoined their class in the library and were soon flanked by their loyal escort who asked no questions, made no attempt to begin a conversation but were there if their friends wanted to talk.

Wendy and Julie kept glancing at Jo as she sat quietly staring at the blank page in front of her and the pencil in her fingers.

"Jo, haven't you any work to do?" the library teacher asked.

Jo shook her head.

"Everyone else seems to be working on some sort of history assignment. Have you finished it?"

"I haven't got it."

"She was away when we got it," Wendy piped up quickly. "She and

Tom have to talk to Mrs Burgess about the topic they want to do before they start."

Julie piped up, "Will it be alright if she helps me today, and I help her later?"

The teacher nodded and Jo roused enough to begin to look up information for her friend.

Tom was perched on the stool at the catalogue terminal making notes of references. When he sensed someone behind him he blanked the screen.

"Need any help, Tom?" he was asked casually.

"No! I'm trying to remember what else I want to look up."

The teacher moved away and Tom went to find the books he'd looked for. From the section he looked at, the teacher had a fair idea of what he was after. It might be for science or for human development, but since he seemed to be busy and wasn't causing trouble, she left him alone.

Info tech was just another period to be endured, though Tom began to concentrate a little on the work. Jo at least found her work folder and scanned through it, showing Wendy what she had done.

At recess, Mike and Will dragged Tom into a game of volleyball, and finally Tom became more animated – as if thumping the ball hard was therapeutic.

Jo sat with her two close friends in a quiet spot under a tree on the edge of the oval. They watched the volleyball game from there and it seemed that Jo did not want to be too far from her brother.

Kelly Phillips, one of the school captains saw the little group and wandered over. He chose to squat down and talk to them. Neither Wendy nor Julie minded his company because he was very good looking. More importantly, he seemed to be trying to get Jo to talk.

"How are you doing, Jo?" he asked her directly.

"I'm okay," Jo said, not looking at him.

"I'm glad you found your brother," Kelly said next and received only a shrug from Jo.

"I met him the other week, decent bloke. Took me a while to figure out he was your brother."

Still no reaction.

"You know, if he'd been my brother, I think I would have done the same."

Jo turned her head to face the senior student. His comment surprised her.

"Of course, if I had," Kelly continued blithely. "Scott wouldn't have just chewed me out. He would have had my head served up on a platter for breakfast."

A faint smile of amusement appeared on Jo's face.

"How is your brother?" Kelly asked, now that he had her attention. He was surprised at her answer.

"I don't know!" The smile disappeared and Jo burst into tears.

"No one will tell us anything. The hospital won't tell us anything. They won't let us see him."

The reason for Jo's manner was now obvious, especially to Wendy who knew how close Ted, Tom and Jo were.

"Is there anyone you know who might be able to find out something?" Kelly asked. He was considering calling them and insisting on having information.

"I could call Dad," Wendy said at once.

"What's your Dad do?"

"Well if you met Ted Dwyer the other week, you probably met Dad too," Wendy grinned. "Inspector Kent."

Kelly's eyes widened as he took in that information.

"Maybe you should," Kelly suggested. "Ask at the office, if you explain why, I'm sure they will let you use the phone. I'll stay here."

Shortly before the end of recess, Wendy returned. She was pleased to see Jo looking a little better and talking back to the senior student.

"Dad hasn't heard anything. The hospital will ring him later, after the doctors have seen your brother again. I'll ring again later."

"Thanks, Wen," Jo said, looking as if she now had some hope.

Wendy was called up to the student foyer during science and was given a message to ring her father. She dialled as fast as possible and waited impatiently for her father to answer.

"Dad, what's the news?"

"You can tell Tom and Jo that Ted is conscious and well enough to be returned to a normal ward. They can visit him for a short time after school. I will pick them up."

"So he's going to be okay?"

Her father hesitated a moment. "He's going to need some time to rest up," Kent told her. "He has a mild concussion, and a few other problems other than being dehydrated and starved."

"Can I tell Tom and Jo all that?"

"Just keep quiet on the 'other problems' for now. They may turn out to be nothing."

"Thanks, Dad. This might help put a little life back in Tom and Jo."

Devin Rhodes ignored the small whispering group. His keen hearing had caught a few words of the conversation and he realised that Tom and Jo were getting some good news.

The group separated after a few minutes and all of them began to work better. He paused to wonder if the Dwyers would be settling down for a while.

Inspector Kent gave his children a head signal hint to wait outside the private ward where Ted Dwyer now rested. He nodded to the policeman on duty outside and pushed the door open and ushered Tom and Jo before him.

Ted seemed to be dozing and he still had a drip attached to his arm.

Jo glanced at the Inspector before perching on a chair next to the bed and staring at her brother's pale face. Ted roused and realised he had visitors.

"Jo. Tom." He greeted with a voice that was very hoarse.

Jo quickly offered him a sip of water from the glass beside the bed.

"Ted!" Jo leant over and hugged him, and felt her big brother return it. Ted collected Tom with his other arm and hugged him too.

"Thank you both," Ted whispered. He knew that Tom and Jo had found him. He was not going to berate them for putting themselves in danger. He would have done the same for them.

"Are you all right?" he asked them.

"We are now. Get better quick, bro."

"I intend to," Ted assured her. "But you and Tom had better not try any more heroics. And behave yourselves at school. I'm trusting you."

"We'll behave for a bit," Tom promised with a faint grin.

"You can't stay long today," Kent reminded Tom and Jo. "Your brother needs to rest. You can come again tomorrow."

The three Dwyers hugged again and said their goodbyes.

Tom and Jo seemed more relaxed after the short visit and he was sure that Constable Dwyer would be equally improved. Wendy was right. The three Dwyers needed to know that the other parts were well.

Ted Dwyer's first question had been about the welfare of his younger siblings. Kent had needed to reassure him, before he was able to get a report from him. The report had confirmed his theory of where he'd been attacked, but Dwyer hadn't seen his attacker. Ted felt sure it could not have been his uncle.

Kent wished he could tell what Ted was thinking when he heard what else had been found in the building where he'd been held prisoner, but his mind seemed to dwell on the fact that his uncle had kept him in a state that might have killed him.

Chapter 17

It was a marvellous evening at Kath Daniels house when Tom and Jo came home from school and found Ted there, talking to her. Tom and Jo dropped their bags and raced over to Ted, ignoring the restrictions about sliding on Kath Daniel's polished wood floors.

"Are you better, properly?" Jo asked first.

"Are you still so weak that I can beat you at arm wrestling?" Tom followed.

"Well enough to beat you," Ted promised. "I've got two weeks sick leave. I thought it would be good for us all to go bush for a week – have a change of scene."

"Will our school let us?" Jo asked.

"Too bad if they don't," Ted said. "For once, I don't care. You'll just have to work harder the week after."

"Where will we be going?" Tom wanted to know. It had been ages since the three of them had gone away together. Besides, it would be a relief not to be under what he privately considered 'house arrest'.

They left the next day after school and travelled north-west, past Bendigo to a small isolated farming area. When they stopped at dusk, they were in a tiny town called Tamboora.

Ted had arranged for them to stay at a bed and breakfast place and whilst his sister and brother were settling in and getting to know their hosts, he used the phone there to report to the nearest police station. The nearest one was ten miles away at Rocky Falls.

Ted didn't want to worry Tom and Jo, but he had been instructed to report regularly and to be alert for anything suspicious. He hoped they had made a clean departure, but he wouldn't be surprised if his uncle had discovered where they were staying and had a watch on it.

One way or another, this holiday was what he needed to think certain things through in his mind. Particularly some odd things that his aunt had said earlier in the day when he had phoned her to check she was okay. In fact, his choice of destination had been influenced by that conversation.

It would have amused Tom if he had known that his sudden departure for a week's holiday had seriously annoyed Fred Jackson.

For all of the week while Ted was in hospital, Jackson's mate Tyson, had been taking every opportunity to needle Tom. He hadn't been told to stay away from Tom, though Tom usually kept away from him.

However, knowing he was going to be away for a week, Tom had chosen to have words with Tyson on the way to the gate.

"You just go and tell Fred to nick off and do his own dirty work, Tyson. While you are at it, tell him to warn his dad to keep his nose clean. The police know Fred's old man is friends with our uncle – so they'll be looking for him too."

Tom hadn't waited around to see Tyson scuttle off to where Jackson lived and tell him what Tom had said. The message angered Jackson so much, that he decided to return to school and confront Tom Dwyer himself.

However, Fred had been absent since he'd got Tom and Jo suspended and when he returned to class with neither note nor medical certificate he was warned that if he so much as took an hour off school for the rest of the year (without proper reason) –he'd be asked to leave the school.

Jackson had to grit his teeth and agree to the condition. He was being paid well to watch the Dwyer kids – and cause trouble for them. In fact, he had trouble planned for that very school day. It was too late when he realised Tom and Jo weren't at school and Tyson heard they would be away a week.

Ted led his brother and sister on a walk up to the top of the falls. It was a new experience for both, as they only remembered living in an inner city suburb.

"Do you remember living anywhere but Footscray?" Ted asked his siblings.

"No," was Tom's prompt answer. "Did we?"

"Yeah."

The admission was bringing to mind painful memories.

"Where" Jo asked.

"In town where we are staying. We were all born there."

"Really? You never told us that before," Jo looked interested.

"Too many memories," Ted admitted to her. He seemed to be engrossed in the magnificent view.

Tom was staring at the water as it plunged two hundred feet to the base of the rock wall. Jo found a rock to sit on and considered her eldest brother. She sensed something in his manner.

"I don't remember the town," Jo admitted. "How old was I when we left?"

"About three, Tom was four…"

Ted stopped talking for a while, but finally went on. "Dad…Dad died. Mum had to go back to work to support us. Then she lost her job. That's when uncle turned up. I didn't know we had an uncle. He said – Dad and he had been estranged for years. He wanted to be friends again, but Dad hadn't. He said – he couldn't let his kin suffer and if we came back to the city with him, Mum would have more chances of better jobs. So that's why we moved."

Tom shrugged. "Maybe that's why he doesn't like us. He didn't like dad."

Ted remembered different things, but he had been older, and his dad had promised to come back. Uncle Ed had understood his anger and given him man-to-man talks – what he needed at that age. Uncle Ed had helped his mother; to move, to settle into a house he'd rented and to find a job to support her family. She had worked very hard too.

"How did Dad die?" Tom asked, still not looking at anyone.

Jo wondered if he was feeling the lack of a father. Ted had always filled that role for her. She was beginning to want to know what her mother had been like – she really couldn't recall her, except from a photo she had.

"Car accident, somewhere north."

"Why did you bring us here?" Tom demanded. "I don't like all this open space."

What had prompted him to come, Ted wondered. Should he tell them what their aunt had said? They deserved to know.

"I spoke to Aunt Hilda before we left. I wanted to know she was all right."

He didn't notice the guilty looks that passed between Tom and Jo. They hadn't once thought of their aunt.

"She couldn't understand why he'd try to hurt us since he had been so insistent that he take us in and how inseparable he and I had been at first. We were a surprise to her because uncle had never mentioned to her that he had a brother. She was thrilled though; she wanted children but couldn't have any."

"Did they ever live around here?" Tom asked.

"No."

"Good."

"Were Mum and Dad born around here?"

"Mum was. Dad, I don't think so. He travelled a lot."

"Then there would be people around here who would have known Mum?" Jo insisted. "I can sort of remember her, I think."

Jo had a small photo of her mother, but it was still at Aunt Hilda's house.

"Yes, people here might remember her. What do you want to know?"

"Am I like her or Dad?" Jo said thoughtfully.

"You do look like her, Jo, though I got so used to her looking tired and worn out - well that's how I remember her."

"And Dad, what was he like? How do you remember him?" Tom asked, now looking at Ted.

Ted didn't want to answer that. "He went away!"

"Well, I don't miss him," Tom said stonily. "You've been all the father I ever wanted. I respect you. You have always been there for us. I don't need him!"

Jo felt the need to change the subject. "So, do we have any other relatives here?"

"No, Mum was an only child and Dad never mentioned anyone."

"Perhaps he was right in not having anything to do with Uncle," Jo said aloud. "Were Dad and Mum married here?"

Tom looked thoughtfully at Jo. He had a good idea why she had asked.

"Yes. Why?"

"Family history," Jo shrugged. "We've never really talked about our family. I might just decide to look at ours – while we're here. We might have more distant relatives."

Ted felt better in the light of Jo's enthusiasm.

"Where did we used to live? Is the place still there?"

Tom had become more interested.

"Yes, we drove past it coming up here."

"Can we see it?" Jo begged.

"I don't know who lives there now. We can't just go barging up to the door and ask to look around."

"Just the outside," Tom clarified.

"Please," Jo urged.

"That's it. The place with the rose bushes out the front. It hasn't changed much."

Tom eyed the house. He was trying to recall being there. Jo saw the large yard behind it. The house was the last in a row of houses. All were on large blocks, but the end one had more space. Someone was driving a tractor beyond the yard.

"Come on, let's go" Ted urged. He tried to shepherd his siblings back into the car where it was parked on the opposite side of the road.

A car came along the road and turned into the drive of the house with the roses. A woman got out, saw them and smiled. "Looking for someone?" she asked in a friendly tone.

"No thanks. Just looking at the house," Ted called back.

The woman seemed to be studying him. Ted smiled, thinking she was memorising his face in case something happened. Then she seemed to see Tom and Jo. Was it his imagination or did the woman suddenly turn pale? The smile had gone.

"Ted? Ted Dwyer?" The woman found her voice.

Ted smiled.

"Yes, and Tom and Jo. I didn't think anyone would remember us. We used to live here once."

"I – I know," the woman stammered. "Adele was my friend since school, but I'd heard that you … I didn't think you would ever come back here. Come in – tell me how you've been."

Tom and Jo were keen. Ted sighed and agreed.

"Thank you. I think I remember you," Ted said. "Here, let me carry some parcels in. Tom, Jo – lend a hand."

"Ros Grant," the woman named herself.

"Of course, Aunt Ros. How's Uncle Jack?"

"Still the same. Just older and gruffer. Stan is in the army. Based around Darwin somewhere. He's just had his second child, another boy. What do you do now, Ted."

"I joined the police force. I'm based at South Melbourne," Ted told her.

They carried the boxes and bags through the front parlour and into the kitchen.

"I'll just put the kettle on," Ros Grant said automatically. "And I'll pop out and tell Jack you're here."

Whilst Ros Grant was outside, Ted found the cups, saucers, tea, coffee and sugar.

"You must be a great help to Adele," Ros commented on her return.

"I did what I could," Ted shrugged. "Didn't you hear that she had passed away?"

"Yes, of course, I did know. Your uncle wrote to us and let us know."

Ted sensed something strange about her answer.

"Yeah," a gruff voice spoke from the back doorway. "He told us you were all dead. As if we weren't good enough for you anymore. Glad ter see he was wrong. How are you, boy?"

Jo giggled, hearing Ted called 'boy' and being slapped on the back. Jack looked then at Jo.

"Well, this must be Jo. You are Adele all over again. Isn't she luv?"

"Yes, she's very like Adele was at the same age. Tom, though, I'm not sure who he takes after but Ted is Ralph to a 't'."

Ros looked thoughtful.

"A Dwyer though, no doubt," Jack proclaimed, studying Tom. "No mistaking the family resemblance – reminds me of young Ted here. Nothing like that so-called brother that turned up to get you. I couldn't come to him at all. Though it was good of him to come and help you at such a difficult time."

Jack's glance at Ted was like an apology for bringing up an old argument.

"You knew our Dad well, did you Mr Grant?" Tom asked.

"Jack, me boy, call me Jack or Uncle Jack if you like."

"Jack," Tom tried the name.

"You could say I knew him well. We were in the army together. National service. Missed out on the war in 'Nam, though."

"Did he ever mention if he had a brother?" Tom asked.

"No, never a word. That's why I was so surprised when the guy turned up. I didn't say much because young Ted really took to him, almost as if he knew him."

 Ted made no comment.

"Why don't you all stay for tea," Jack invited. "We can manage something, can't we luv?"

Ros Grant nodded, "Of course we can."

"Good, 'cos I've got to finish ploughing that paddock out back. Want to give me a hand, young Ted? You used to like driving the tractor."

Jack winked at Tom.

"He wasn't really old enough to be meant to!"

"Any chance I could try?" Tom asked, watching Ted for his reaction.

Ted snorted. "Yeah, why not? Who's to know? What about you, Jo?"

"I was thinking of baking a cake," Ros said quickly.

"Mmm, could I help?" Jo asked at once, turning to wink at Tom when no one else would see.

She was waiting a chance to talk to Aunt Ros about things – including the uncle that no one knew they had.

Ted watched Tom carefully driving the tractor.

"What's this about being told we were all dead," Ted asked Jack when Tom was too far away to hear.

"Just that. We had a brief 'Sorry to inform you' letter from Edward Dwyer Esq. I regret to inform you – blah blah – you all died in a car accident. As you were friends of the family, I thought you would like to know. Is that how your mother died?"

Jack was also watching Tom.

"No! She had pneumonia, but no realised it until too late. She just kept on working long hours so she could support us. She hated being grateful for anyone's charity."

"She was a great one for giving it though," Jack remembered. "The town sure missed her help when she moved to Melbourne."

Jack was silent for a long time.

"You sure gave the wife a turn, showing up."

"Well, if you thought we were dead, I can understand that. I wonder why he told you that though."

"Thing is," Jack went on. "This is something I never even told the wife. But, a couple of years after I heard about, well, you being dead, I saw a man, a tramp. I would swear on anything that it was Ralph Dwyer."

"Did you talk to him," Ted asked intently, turning to face Jack.

Jack looked uncomfortably like he was going to cry.

"Yes, I did. He was wandering in his wits, but he asked about Adele and the rest of you. I told him what I'd been told. He didn't seem to understand, but the next day – a package arrived with a letter. He'd deeded the house to me and asked me to keep the package safe until he returned. I can't quite think where it is now, but I will get it to you when I find it. I told Ros that the deeds had come from a lawyer somewhere."

"Do you think he might still be alive?" Ted asked, not daring to hope.

"A couple of days later, a hobo walked in front of a train."

Jack's voice was rough from controlling the memory. Ted felt tears in his own eyes and an unreasoning anger at his uncle Edward.

"It wasn't your fault, Jack," Ted said in a voice that was none too steady. "Uncle or not, he must really have hated my father to do what he did."

Tom brought the tractor to a halt in front of Ted.

"How'd I do?" Tom was grinning.

"Too good, you young hooligan," Ted admonished. "You'll be thinking you can borrow my car next. Let me see if I can do better."

Ted helped Tom down then climbed into the seat and started to move off.

"The rows are a bit wobbly," Tom admitted. "But that was just so cool. I wouldn't be allowed to do that at home."

Ted found the old skill coming back and hardly had to think about what he was doing. That was as well, because his mind was full on questions. So he began to review what he had been told and what he knew.

Firstly, he had been told his father was dead when he wasn't. An uncle no one knew about turns up and whisks them off. So, even if his father had come back – as he had – he would not know where they were. Then the town is told they were all dead – no doubt to sever all contact between the town and his family. Then his father finally returns and is told his family is dead and gone. So, Ralph Dwyer goes off and fetches something from somewhere, seemingly intending to return – but then apparently kills himself.

The first obvious conclusion was that Uncle Edward had lied to everyone all along the way – but why? If he hated Ralph Dwyer so much – why go to such lengths? Why didn't he simply kill Ralph? Why go to so much bother 'helping' his family?

Who was Edward Dwyer if he was not Ralph's brother? Nothing made sense.

Ted turned his full attention to the ploughing and let the questions drift around in the back of his mind.

Jo took a liking to Ros Grant and plied her with questions about her mother as they were making the cake. Then as it was cooking, Ros brought out her photo albums and showed Jo photos of her mother's wedding and even some of her, Tom and Ted as babies.

Jo finally changed the focus of her questions to her father. She heard how her mother had met him at a dance when he was working for a time in the area.

"Ralph was a proper gentleman," Ros told Jo. "I never was quite sure what he did for a living. He travelled a lot. A salesman, probably, because he spent a lot of time talking to farmers."

As if by mutual consent, the topic of the afternoon's chat' were not mentioned at tea time. Ros and Jack talked of town gossip. Most of it bored Tom and Jo but they stayed politely quiet. Ted seemed to remember most of the people talked about and he asked after others. He didn't mention their recent misadventures. As far as the Grants were concerned, the three Dwyers were in town on a holiday.

Chapter 18

On subsequent days, Ted drove out to other local landmarks and even took his siblings fishing in the river. He seemed to relax as Tom and Jo enjoyed learning to do things he had done since he was younger than they were now. Tom, too, seemed to be less tensed by being out in the open.

Jo talked her brother into visiting the little church at Rocky Falls where their parents had been married. They arrived while the visiting priest was in attendance and he allowed them to search the register to find the details of their parents wedding. Jo wrote down everything she could. Her father had given his job as a 'representative' and her mother's was 'waitress'. She then hunted for the details of their christenings and noted them down too.

The priest was an old man and knew the district and its people well. He knew of their mother's people, gave their names to Jo, and showed her to where they were buried in the little cemetery beside the church. Tom just shook his head at his sister's new obsession and shared a grin with his brother.

That day was Friday and Tom and Jo went with Ted when he reported in to the local police station. Ted found that the district Inspector was visiting and had usurped the Sergeant's office.

"A word with you, Constable," Inspector Walton invited, gesturing Ted into the office. "You two, find some mischief to keep yourselves amused."

"You can always offer to wash the patrol car," the duty officer, a young policewoman, Jessie Albright suggested tongue in cheek.

"Na," Jo dismissed the idea with a flick of her hand. "We wouldn't want to pinch someone else's fun."

"Is that," Tom pointed to the closed door, "likely to take long?"

"Who knows?" Constable Albright shrugged. "So how come you two are not in school?"

"Having a rest cure," Jo said casually. "And making sure Ted doesn't over do things."

"And having a break from teachers who think we get into too much mischief as it is," Tom added with a grin.

"Voluntary or not?" Albright teased.

"Voluntary this time," Jo confirmed. "Our previous break was a trifle more – forced."

A fax began to emerge from a printer behind the counter. Albright glanced at it.

"I heard that you rescued your brother," Albright commented, as if reminded of the fact by what she read on the fax.

"Well, we found him," Tom agreed.

"Gutsy work, dangerous though. Next time, leave it to us."

"There had better not be a next time!" Jo said forcefully.

Albright took the fax and knocked on the office door.

"Sir, this just came through. I thought it appropriate to bring in," Albright explained her interruption. She reappeared a moment later.

"So what have you been doing while you've been here?" Albright asked.

"Rediscovering our roots," Jo answered immediately. "We'd forgotten we were born here."

"Like it here?"

"It's a bit too open for me," Tom admitted. "We've turned into city brats, I think."

"Well, so was I until I was posted here, but I love it."

Albright went on to talk about the things she liked about working in Rocky Falls.

"Sit!" Inspector Walton invited, as he sat back behind the sergeant's desk.

"I have the results of that inquiry you instigated," Walton got right to the point. "Not conclusive."

"What did you find, Sir?"

"The body of the hobo was badly mangled. It was identified by an Edward Dwyer, as that of his brother, Ralph. I understand that the identification was based on the clothing the deceased was wearing. The autopsy found evidence of chronic alcoholism."

"Were the autopsy results compared to army medical records?" Ted asked.

"The deceased had no teeth and no dentures were found," Walton said. "So we couldn't compare them with the army dental records."

"Fingerprints?"

The Inspector merely shook his head. "As I said, we had to take the brother's word as to the identity."

At that moment there was a knock at the office door.

"Come in," Walton called.

The constable brought in a fax and handed it to Walton.

Walton scanned it quickly to see why the constable had considered it important enough to bring in. When he finished, he handed it to Ted.

Ted read the report of the arrest of his uncle and two accomplices.

"That's excellent news, Sir," Ted referred to the fax. "As for the other business, there doesn't seem to be anything else I can do."

Walton eyed the constable for a long moment. "This might not be anything, but I requested not just medical records for Ralph Dwyer. His file has no entries after 1960. That would be when his two years national service finished. I would have expected a date of his demobbing."

"Can I read the file?" Ted asked.

Walton pushed a manila folder at him.

"The details are meant to be confidential," Walters warned.

Ted nodded and scan read the file. After doing basic training, Ralph Dwyer had twelve months in a light infantry battalion and was then transferred to the military police. There were mentions of two service medals, but little else. No next of kin was recorded.

"Thank you, Sir," Ted handed the file back. His mind retained the details, including his Father's date of birth and place of birth. Jo would be interested in that as much as he was. He'd like to get a copy of his father's birth certificate, but that wouldn't show if he had younger siblings.

"When do you leave?" Walton asked.

"Might go tomorrow," Ted decided. "Or Sunday. I don't think I should keep Tom and Jo away from school too long, but they needed this break as much as I did."

"I heard what they did, finding you. Glad they found you, but I can't approve of their methods."

"I share your sentiments, Sir," Ted agreed, tactfully. It seemed to be the correct answer, as the Inspector nodded and waved a hand in his dismissal.

"Off you go, take those two young devils with you. Buy them a milkshake or something to celebrate!"

Ted decided to follow the suggestion.

Chapter 19

Tom and Jo returned to school full of good intentions for working hard and making up for missed work. They had arbitrarily decided that their uncle was a fake and deserved no loyalty or concern from them. And of course, now that he was in jail, they had nothing to fear from him.

It wasn't conscious on their part, but they no longer had the urge to play up at school, because they were no longer rebelling against conditions at home.

Ted had decided that they should continue to stay with Kath Daniels. She admitted to enjoying their company.

The first day back, Ted had taken Tom and Jo back to their uncle's house and collected all their stuff from their bedrooms. Stuff they didn't need often was to be boxed up and stored.

Ted thought long and hard about moving himself out, before deciding that he would. His concern was for his aunt, living alone in the house without an income.

"I've already decided, Ted dear," she said calmly. "I'm going to move my things out of here and live with my sister. There isn't a great deal here that means anything to me. I am going to go back to school to refresh my qualifications and then I will be able to help my sister and her husband with their business. Really, I'll be fine. With Edward here, I could never break away – now I can. With luck, he'll be away a long time. I won't go back to him and if I get too independent, he won't want me."

"Good for you, Aunt. I don't know how you stood it all these years."

"Oh, he wasn't so bad at first," Hilda Dwyer admitted. "I really did love him. He changed, gradually, but I didn't want to see the changes. I had married him for better and for worse. I eventually learnt that if I acted dumb and dependant, he treated me well enough. Then when he took you in, I felt I had to stay."

Ted gave his aunt a hug of gratitude. "What will you do about the house?" he asked.

"I don't know," Hilda admitted. "Nothing for a while. I plan to see a lawyer, eventually, about a divorce. I'll let them advise me."

"Do you know where the deeds are?" Ted asked. "We should ensure they are safe."

"Edward kept all the papers together. I know that much. I'd guess they will be in his den. I'm sure he kept nothing important in his bedroom. After all, I was allowed in there to keep it tidy."

"I suppose it is paid off?" Ted thought suddenly.

"I … assume so. I never had anything to do with the household bills, except when he gave me money to pay the electricity and water."

"I think, you and I, need to go through Uncle's den and find out the state of affairs."

Ted found the idea of looking in there distasteful. "I'll come back tomorrow, after I drop Tom and Jo at school."

It was not a pleasant feeling, being in Edward Dwyer's den. Ted had stopped thinking of him as his uncle.

"I've never been allowed in here," Hilda Dwyer said quietly. "Even if I do have the spare key."

"Is your feminine inquisitiveness getting active, Aunt Hilda?" Ted tried to lighten his own feelings.

"Not really, but I agree we need to find the house documents. What is the smell in here?"

Ted sniffed. "I'm not sure. I didn't notice it the other day. Where will we start in this mess?"

"It's odd. He insisted the rest of the house be tidy – why did he keep this like it is?" Hilda asked.

"I don't know," Ted said, trying to decide where to look first.

His decision was postponed by the ringing of the doorbell. He went to answer it.

"Sir! What can I do for you?" Ted recognised the officer in charge of the forgery investigation. He had spoken to Inspector Joseph on previous occasions.

"We have a warrant to search the house. We believe we may find the plates for the forged notes here."

"Go for it Sir. I don't think you will find what you are looking for but come and look anyway. I was just about to look through the den for some private papers we need. So, would I be permitted to assist?"

"Constable Dwyer, I believe you are on sick leave. Leave this to us," Joseph advised.

"Will you let me know if you find the deeds to the house?" Ted requested. "I need to know if the house is paid off or not."

"We're here to look for printer's plates, Dwyer," Ted was told, but the Inspector nodded his head in understanding.

After the den, they checked the rest of the house but no plates were found. The detectives doing the search confiscated a number of small items recognised as being stolen, passed over a cache of strong spirits and found a large pile of pornographic magazines. Ted was asked back into the den before they left.

"There are a lot of private papers in the corner in a box," Joseph informed Ted. "We'd like you to go through the box with us."

"Okay, but not in here," Ted agreed.

One of the detectives carried the box out into the kitchen, where Hilda had the kettle hot and offered coffee or tea to the detectives. Only Inspector Joseph accepted.

Ted looked through everything, and sorted the contents onto the table. He found, near the bottom, an old photo of a group of army men. One of the men was Edward Dwyer, another might have been his own father.

Then, surprise of surprises, the deed to the house they were in – in the name of Ralph Dwyer! Soon after that discovery, they found the paid receipt for a post box in Footscray. Ted showed it to the detectives.

"I'll need to look into that," Ted said thoughtfully. "I think all the bills go there. Did you notice the address on the electricity account when you paid it?"

"I have a book. I pay so much each month," Hilda admitted.

The box also contained purchase receipts for some of the electrical items in the house as well as the manuals.

"That's the lot," Ted said finally. "Not much to go on."

"Why didn't you expect us to find the plates here?" Joseph asked Ted.

"I think they might have been here the day I was attacked," Ted said thinking back. "I found a package, wrapped in brown paper, on the desk. I picked it up – it was too heavy to be a wad of printed currency. If Dwyer knew I'd been in here, he'd get it away at once. I thought you might have found more in here – since he was paranoid about keeping us out."

"And the mess?"

"Normal for in here, I think. Maybe I should ask Tom and Jo. I'm sure they have snuck in here a few times when he wasn't around. They were in here the day before he came home last and he often claimed they did."

"Your brother and sister?" Joseph enquired. "Dangerous activity…"

"I think they know that," Ted said stiffly.

"But it didn't stop them?"

"No, but I don't seem to remember how teenagers think anymore."

"Where would they be at the moment? School?"

"Yes. When would you like me to talk to them?"

"As soon as possible," Joseph requested. "It is just possible that they found a hiding place we missed. Vengeful eyes and all that."

"Vengeful," Ted repeated. "Yes, I think that is an apt description. I think they have never liked him. He had me fooled. I'll ring the school – they can wait at the office for us."

Only Inspector Joseph accompanied Ted to the school. The remaining three detectives stayed at the house.

They arrived at the start of lunchtime. Tom and Jo turned up a couple of minutes later. Hendry offered the group the use of his office.

Ted explained what they wanted to know. Two identical smiles of malice appeared on the teenagers' faces.

"Well, he keeps his booze in a hole under the floor, under the table," Jo began at once.

"And his porno magazines in a cupboard next to the window," Tom added.

"We found both those places," Joseph confirmed.

"There's another floor hole under the couch," Tom revealed. "The couch was too heavy for me to move, so I could never get it open to see what was in there."

"And if you look closely at the roof in the corner next to the door, you can see two lines at right angles," Jo went on. "There's a wall blocking that section of the roof. We checked by going up the manhole."

"Is that all you can tell us?" Joseph asked when both students stopped talking.

"I assume you checked the furniture for secret holes," Jo asked. "Tom and I often wondered about that couch."

"Vengeful eyes indeed, Dwyer."

"What's that supposed to mean?" Jo asked.

Ted grinned and explained. "It's like saying 'Hell has no fury like a woman scorned'. There should be a similar saying about teenagers. How's school been this morning?"

"Quiet," Jo answered. "We told Mr Rhodes that we were going to make up for missed time and past idleness. He was quite impressed."

"That's good to hear. Off you go!" Ted instructed.

"Oh, and Fred Jackson has, according to rumour, been told that if he has any more days off this year – he'll be asked to leave the school," Tom grinned.

"You keep away from him, still!" Ted warned.

"We will!" Tom promised.

The hole in the roof proved to be the most interesting. It had a pull down ladder and was secured by a lock hidden in a loose piece of cornice. They still didn't find printers plates, but they did find a large box of forged share certificates and similar documents. Along with the box, was a tin containing a roll of deeds for various properties, made out in different names and a carefully kept account book of what a list of people owed Eddy Dwyer. One name was the owner of the building where Ted was found.

A second roll of documents was for three places owned by Eddy Dawson; the house in Willow Street, the warehouse in Greyson Street and a third place in Port Melbourne.

Chapter 20

Tom and Jo hadn't forgotten Fred Jackson's attempts to get them in trouble. With the help of their friends, they were rarely alone during school hours and with either Ted or Gayle Kent driving them to and from school, they had themselves covered for those times too.

For the first two weeks of their return, it seemed that their precautions were unnecessary. Fred Jackson kept his distance and nothing happened to disturb them. Tom's first inkling of trouble came when he saw a faint smile on Jackson's face one morning as Ten Green students walked out of the maths lab and Ten Silver waited to go in. Jackson's eyes flicked in Tom's direction, but that was all.

The first thing that Tom noticed when they entered the room was that the teacher wasn't Mr Nesbitt. The man was much younger.

"Mr Trogan," Will Kent whispered. "He was here the week you were off."

"What's he like?" Tom whispered back.

"He's ok," Will summarised.

Tom had to agree. He had decided he liked the teacher when a loud bang startled everyone and smoke began to emerge from the metal cupboard where the maths equipment was stored. The foul smell was overpowering.

"Everyone leave your books, and walk outside," Trogan ordered at once.

The smoke detectors had already triggered the fire alarms and other classes were emerging from adjoining classrooms. While classes were marshalling on the oval and students were being counted – the fire brigade arrived.

"I hope this wasn't one of your tricks," Steve Reynolds remarked in an undertone as the watched the activity.

"It certainly wasn't," Tom assured him.

"You went to get the pegboards out," Steve remarked. "Did you notice anything?"

"No."

Reynolds shook his head and moved away.

It didn't take long for the situation to be controlled. All students except for Ten Silver were soon able to return to their rooms. Even with all the windows open in the maths room, it still reeked of the fetid smoke released by the stink bomb. Trogan told his students to sit outside and he went over to confer with the fire officers and the deputy principal. On his return, he modified his lesson and continued it outside. When the bell went, his students were allowed back into the room to collect their books and pencil cases.

The smell was almost gone, but Jo inadvertently breathed in a pocket of the foul air that was trapped in a corner and felt her throat begin to burn. Tom noticed her distress and when he realised she couldn't talk, called the teacher over. Trogan took one look at Jo's pallor and sent Tom to take her to the infirmary.

The nurse told Jo to lie down, but that made her feel worse, so she sat up and breathed oxygen through a facemask for a time. After that, she was given something to drink that soothed and numbed her throat. Tom sat with her, but didn't talk much.

"How are you?" Marcus Hendry asked when he walked into the infirmary.

"Better, thank you," Jo whispered.

"Rather nasty trick, that smoke bomb," Hendry remarked, watching both Jo and her brother. "It was placed for maximum effect and minimum damage. Only one shelf of equipment was damaged and nowhere for the fire to spread. Quite considerate."

Tom didn't miss the innuendo.

"We didn't put it there!" Tom said flatly, meeting Hendry's gaze squarely.

"I hope you didn't," was Hendry's quiet warning as he left the infirmary.

That was the start of a series of incidents that began to plague Ten Silver. Many students began looking speculatively at Tom and Jo. They had changed. They were not as cheerful as normal and the tricks were not funny either.

The tricks seemed designed to waste lesson time – globes were missing from projectors and the spares were broken, equipment was out of place, books muddled up, batteries and power cords missing, messes were made in cupboards and gooey liquids were spilt in odd places.

Finally, Hendry came to address Ten Silver, during the afternoon homeroom time.

"There have been too many incidents happening in rooms used by this class or in rooms last used by this class. The acts of vandalism have to stop. If those responsible don't own up, before the end of the week – this whole class will have detention until we find the culprit."

There was a murmur of resentment and many eyes turned in the direction of Tom and Jo. The Dwyers were aware of what their classmates thought, but this time they were seriously trying to work. The incidents annoyed them as much as they did the rest of the class. Hendry caught Tom's eye as the class was leaving.

"I'd like to talk to you and Jo tomorrow at first break."

Tom nodded and followed his classmates out. He refrained from asking 'why'. He could guess.

"What do you think, Devin?" Marcus Hendry asked the Ten Silver homeroom teacher.

The two teachers were alone in the staff room. "Do you think Tom and Jo are behind these latest acts of vandalism? They have had a rough trot lately."

"I'm not sure," Devin Rhodes had to admit. "They have been working hard since they came back this time – they weren't before. They aren't as cheerful as they used to be either. Though I must point out, when they played up before, their tricks were meant to make people laugh and were carefully done so as not to harm anyone."

"Well, three of these latest tricks have caused injury, or nearly did," Hendry remarked.

"The first was Jo herself," Rhodes reminded Hendry.

"A miscalculation, perhaps. We have to find the person responsible."

"I agree, but I would wait and see the result of your ultimatum. If Tom and his sister are involved, I am sure they will own up rather than have all their classmates suffer. I don't think they have changed that much."

"How have their classmates reacted to the fact that their uncle is in jail?"

"I haven't heard any untoward remarks from my class, but I have heard comments from others."

"What sort of comments?"

"That crime runs in the family. That they will be or ought to be kicked out of school because their uncle is in jail. That if anything is missing, ask them..."

"How are they taking it?"

"Ignoring it. They have some good friends. Generally, all of Ten Silver like them, in spite or because of their earlier tricks."

"And now?"

"You saw them. They are all beginning to wonder and to treat Tom and Jo as outcasts."

"Could they be reacting to that treatment and to the publicity about their uncle?"

Devin shrugged. "Do you want me to talk to them?"

"Leave it with me," Hendry decided.

"Come in," Hendry invited, keeping his tone friendly.

Tom and Jo were not looking rebellious nor defiant – merely resigned.

"Have a seat."

Tom and Jo sat in the two chairs and slumped back, waiting for Hendry to speak.

"I've had good reports of the work you've done lately," he began.

"We've been trying," Jo confirmed. "Really."

"It shows. You are certainly proving what you are capable of. Why did you decide to start to work?"

That was not an easy question to answer.

"Because now we can," Jo answered finally.

Hendry thought about her answer. "You mean, now that your uncle is in prison?"

Jo nodded.

"How do you feel about him being in prison?"

"It's where he belongs!" Tom said.

"From what I've read, I have to agree with you. So were your little sprees of tricks when he was around, or when he wasn't? Your brother mentioned that he was often away."

Neither Tom nor Jo looked at him. Both were thinking, that Hendry was about to start blaming them for the latest pranks.

"When he was around," Jo answered.

"Why was that?"

"Because playing tricks made us feel better," Jo told him.

"Even when you got detention?"

"Yeah," Tom agreed. "At least then we were able to catch up on some homework or assignments."

Hendry betrayed his surprise. "You could have come to me or to one of your teachers and explained the trouble."

Tom looked up with a hint of anger in his expression. "What could you do? Talk to Uncle? You know what he said about us and how nice and civilised he acts when he wants to. We did tell our teachers why we couldn't do our work. One day he really did lock us outside until after dark. He often made us do work around the place without allowing us time to do our schoolwork and we really couldn't work in our rooms. He keeps low wattage globes in our lights and it's too dull to work in. And he turns our lights out at ten o'clock. No one ever believed us so we gave up trying."

"Your brother…"

"Ted wasn't around all the time and uncle was always nice to him," Jo butted in. "At least he finally knows what the bastard is really like."

"So detention was a chosen option," Hendry probed further. "You had fun getting it and you got to do your work…"

"And if it was after school, it kept us out with a reason he couldn't stop – until after he left for work," Tom added.

"Besides, he was relatively easier to live with if he thought we were in trouble at school."

Hendry nodded. "I see." He did, all too clearly.

"I've heard that some students are giving you a hard time because your uncle is in prison."

"We ignore the idiots," Tom growled. "They don't know what they are talking about."

"Does it annoy you?"

"A little," Tom admitted.

"Jo?"

"Alright – a lot!" Jo snapped. "What can you possibly do about it? If we complained to a teacher, they'd just tell us to ignore it anyway."

"We could talk to the worst offenders," Hendry suggested.

"Huh!" Tom snorted.

"Are you getting much of it from your classmates?"

"Not too much," Jo told him. "They've been pretty good about it."

"So, now we have someone playing tricks, mainly aimed at Ten Silver." Hendry kept his tone casual.

"What do you think – are these tricks funny?"

"NO!" Jo said with real passion. "They're vile. Julie almost broke her arm because of one of them. Other people could have been hurt too. Most are straight out vandalism."

"Tom?"

"If I'd been in no mood to work, I might have enjoyed the batteries or globes and stuff missing from equipment, and the other disruptions to class, but we didn't do any of it!"

"Can you see how it looks?" Hendry asked them. "You've both got long pages of records of playing tricks, of disrupting class, of detention – ever since you've been here. Do you want me to read out the details?"

Tom shook his head.

"You have very inventive minds. How can we believe you aren't playing these tricks now? Before, it seems you were playing tricks when you were angry or upset by your uncle – now you could be playing tricks because you are angry or upset by the way people are treating you because of your uncle being in prison."

"No …" Jo denied the accusation. She tried to control the tears in her eyes.

"Jo, no one is going to listen. Everyone thinks it's us." Tom told his sister.

"Look, Sir. If you want a scapegoat – go ahead blame us! We don't care! That way, at least the rest of our class won't get detention."

"Are you admitting to all the incidents?"

"No, we bloody well aren't," Tom swore, he didn't care what Hendry would say about swearing at him. "But if … all of our class are down on us because of your threat of detention. I don't want to take the rap someone else's actions but … I can't take everyone hating us. If they think we owned up to stop them having detention, they won't hate us."

Tom was trying not to break down and cry himself. "And you don't even know that it's someone in Ten Silver doing it."

Hendry decided that he had got more from this session with the Dwyers than he had bargained for. Hopefully he hadn't pushed them too far. They were under a lot of stress at the moment. However, if they had not admitted guilt by now – they were telling the truth.

"Stay a while, will you?" Hendry asked them quietly. He left his office but didn't go far.

He could hear Tom talking to Jo.

"If we hadn't promised Ted we would stay at school and work hard, I'd walk out right now and never come back!"

"Fred bloody Jackson would like that, wouldn't he?" Jo agreed sourly. "Do you really want to give him the satisfaction?"

"No!" Tom growled. "I'd like to punch his face again. He's acting Mr Perfect and badmouthing us to all his mates and anyone else who will listen."

Principal Scott came into the room about half an hour later. He sat at Hendry's desk and watched them for a while before speaking.

"I was on my way here to tell you I didn't believe your story of innocence," he told them baldly. "Not with almost four years of pranks to your credit…"

Tom and Jo slumped back into their chairs, with tears threatening to overwhelm them.

"But, there's been an incident. What lesson are you meant to be in now?"

"Geography," Tom said quietly.

"Yes, indeed," Scott went on. "Room 4.07, right?"

"Yes, Sir."

"Someone has used texta to scribble over a lot of maps on the map hanger. They also used your art signature, Jo. Colossal conceit, like telling all the staff that they are fools. Do you think I'm a fool?"

"No," Jo whispered, feeling sick.

"That's good, because I am not blaming you for the vandalism."

Jo looked up. Her eyes were red and watery.

"Tim Joyce has assured me that there was no damage to the maps at the start of the lesson before. He had looked through the rack for a particular chart he wanted. Now, I know where both of you have been since the end of second period, so the question is – who is responsible?"

When neither Tom nor Jo had an answer, Scott spoke again.

"I appreciate that you may not want to accuse anyone without proof, but this matter is too serious – for everyone – it has to be stopped."

Still no answer.

"Has Fred Jackson been keeping away from you?"

"Yes," Tom had to admit.

"What about his mates?"

"We keep away from them too," Tom stated.

"When we can," Jo qualified.

"Who in particular?" Scott probed.

"Tyson's the main one," Tom mentioned. "But…" He mentioned a few other names.

Jo added a few names of girls. "And sometimes they get their younger siblings to annoy us."

Scott had quickly jotted down the list of names.

"I wish you had come to me about this before," he told them. "Or at least to your home room teacher. This kind of bullying isn't permitted, any more than physical bullying."

"It's petty," Jo said.

"Compared to what? If it is affecting your work, your classmates, and your peace of mind – I wouldn't call it petty. If you were expelled because of these acts – would that be petty?"

Jo shook her head.

"I think it would be best if you were to go to the library until the end of this period and rejoin your class at the start of the next lesson. I will give you a permission slip. Come back here at the start of lunch."

Tom took the permission slip and a very subdued pair of students went across to the library. The staff member at the desk made no comment other than the suggestion of finding somewhere quiet to study.

"Where were you at recess?" Wendy hissed at Jo as they entered their classroom for English.

"Up at the office," Jo told her friend.

Wendy sighed with relief. "So they can't blame you for the maps."

"No, thank goodness. Scott was all set to disbelieve us, but Mr Joyce swore the maps were okay at the start of period two."

"And of course, you weren't there in period three!" Wendy cheered. "What are they going to do?"

"Find out who is doing all the things."

"Jackson is my bet," Will Kent added his belief. "His class had Geography in period two. And since your uncle was arrested, his old man has been watched and questioned."

"Did your Dad tell you that?" Jo asked.

"Not exactly. I overheard him talking to Mum."

"I don't know what they are going to do," Jo said. "But we have to go back at the start of lunch."

"Do they think you are guilty or what?" Will demanded.

"No, but it was close. The geography incident was the decider. I'll let you know what the outcome is."

"How can you be so cheerful about it?" Wendy said angrily, as they walked to where Gayle Kent parked her car.

"Well, you have to admit, it's brilliant, well, clever anyway," Jo argued.

"What's so clever about being supervised at both breaks and dumped into a class with no friends? Sounds like punishment to me!"

"But we know it's not," Jo insisted.

"Can I tell the rest of the class that?" Wendy asked.

Jo shook her head. "You can tell Will, Julie and Mike, that's all. I trust you and them."

"So what's the idea behind all this?"

"Basically, we aren't going to be where the idiots pulling the pranks expect us to be. We'll be at homeroom with Ten Silver, but doing lessons with Ten Red for the next week."

"Why Ten Red?"

"Because as best as we can tell, none of Fred Jackson's flunkeys are in Ten Red," Jo explained.

"So what do they expect?"

"With luck, the trouble makers will keep acting, assuming we are where we are meant to be, and the teachers will have proof that it couldn't be us."

"Okay, but what if this little charade is discovered?" Wendy asked.

"Opinion on that is mixed. They would have to work out a new schedule for their tricks and possibly stop for a while."

"But how will that help catch the real culprits?"

"It's my guess that the teachers will be stepping up security indoors during breaks," Jo suggested. "Since Scott made such a point of it over the intercom this afternoon."

"What about this supervision business," Wendy skipped to the other part of the issue.

"It's extra protection for us," Jo explained.

"One of us will be out and about at each break. The other will be hiding in the little room off the staff room. That's where we will need help from you, Will, Mike and Julie. People are so used to seeing us together, that if they see Tom, they'll assume I'm around and vice versa. And if they see you and Julie, they'll also assume I'm not far off. But at the same time, if there is a period when they can't see me, they'll reason that the teachers won't have seen me either for a time and assume they can sneak in somewhere and pull a prank."

"And you think all that is amusing? You have a warped sense of humour, Jo Dwyer."

"It is funny. The way it looks, no one believes us and we appear to be one step away from major trouble. Tom and I both think that if Fred is behind all this, he will step up the pressure – and be caught out."

"And expelled, I hope," Wendy wished fervently.

"Yeah!" Jo agreed.

Chapter 21

"Why didn't you tell me what was happening at school?" Ted chided his siblings.

"We told you about the stink bomb," Tom reminded him.

They hadn't a choice about that. Jo had felt dreadful for a week before her throat got better.

"And nothing after that," Ted countered. "If Fred Jackson is behind all this – I want to know!"

"Fred has been scrupulously avoiding us and we have been avoiding him and his mates," Tom said patiently.

"Ted, we swear, we have not been playing tricks. We have been working hard and handing our work in on time and we've been allowed to redo some of our substandard assignments," Jo told her elder brother.

"The teachers believe us," Tom said, ignoring how close the decision had been to disbelief. "They intend to catch the real culprits and we agreed to work it the way they decided. It looks like we are in big trouble and Fred won't think we dobbed on him."

"Either way, Jackson won't like you," Ted sighed.

"What's new?" Tom scowled.

"The restraining order is still valid for another year and a half," Ted reminded his siblings. "Keep watching out for him. He'll be in strife if it is proved that he instigated the pranks to get you in trouble."

Tom and Jo nodded.

"And tell me if this charade gets too much for you," Ted insisted. "Remember, we're Dwyers, we stick together."

"So you have discounted uncle?" Tom picked up.

"Yes. It seems his real name is Eugene Edward Dixon, aka Edward Dawson, aka Edward Dwyer."

"How did you discover that?" Jo asked.

"When the forgery guys searched the house, they found a box of documents. In there was a photo of an army group. The men in the photo were finally identified. One was the man we called uncle."

Jo, slipping out of the staff room after lunch break, heard the shouting.

Fred Jackson was in full bellow.

"You can't do this to me you fu… morons. I haven't done anything. I've abided by the conditions you set and I've stayed away from the little cretins."

The teacher's voice was inaudible. They didn't shout their private conversations. As much as she wanted to know the details, she kept going. If Jackson saw her around, he'd blame her for his trouble.

Jo passed Wendy enroute to their different classes. "Jackson is up at the office, yelling the place down," she said quickly.

"Tyson and Pearce were caught in the art room at lunch time," Wendy related her own news. "And Mike saw Hendry talking to Gilly and Dowd. I hope this means that your exile is almost over."

"So do I," Jo said fervently.

The humour of the situation had quickly palled. No one in Ten Red were being more than passingly civil to them and being in the staff room annex at alternate breaks made her feel like she was really in trouble. Not all the staff knew of the true reason for her presence. She was sure that Tom also had to put up with the knowing glances. At least today, when Kelly Phillips had joined her, it hadn't been so bad.

It may not have occurred to the teachers that certain news travels very fast around the school. There had been no announcement, but at the start of the next lesson, Tom and Jo were surprised when one of the students in Ten Red approached and actually spoke to them.

"Heard Tyson was caught in the art room," the boy said. "He was uncapping paint tubes and messing the cupboard."

Tom smiled maliciously. "Glad I'm in Ten Red at the moment. I might have had to clean up the mess."

The other boy grinned too. "I reckon you out foxed that lout, huh?"

"Serves him right," Tom muttered.

"Our home room teacher said not to mention you were in our lessons. Now I know why. I couldn't have done it. You're all right Dwyer."

"Thanks!" Tom grinned wider.

The confidential conversation between Scott, Hendry and the Dwyers (which included Ted Dwyer as guardian of Tom and Jo), took place well after most of the staff and students had departed.

"What we discuss here is not to be spread around the school," Scott stared hard at Tom and Jo.

"I decided, given the situation over the past weeks, that certain information needed to be shared. I don't know how much you have been told about the incidents that were occurring over the past month," Scott was looking at Ted.

"Some," Ted admitted, not sure he knew everything.

"The incidents were becoming progressively more damaging to property and dangerous to people. We were able to clear Tom and Jo of any complicity and with their cooperation, we caught the students who were responsible. I really must commend them for tolerating a difficult set of circumstances and still showing a remarkable improvement in their work."

Ted smiled at Tom and then Jo.

Scott continued. "The ring leader was Fred Jackson, although he was conspicuously behaving himself. He planned the acts of vandalism and encouraged other students to carry them out. We learnt from talking to these students, that it was Jackson's intention to have the blame laid on Tom and Jo, a reasonable possibility, given their record to date. All of Jackson's accomplices have been identified and warned and have received appropriate punishment. Jackson has been told he is no longer welcome here. It is clear though that he is harbouring anger against Tom and Jo."

"I've already spoken to them about that," Ted assured the principal. "But I am glad you are also aware of the situation."

"There is a point we would like to stress," Hendry spoke for the first time and he was looking at the two students. "We are aware that you have trouble on a personal front. We hope, that if it begins to affect your work again, that you come to us. We have options available to help you cope."

"We'll think about it," Tom answered.

"We mean what we said," Scott stressed. "And we also wish to avoid any of your own antics in the future."

"We'll behave ourselves between now and the last day of school,"

Jo promised.

Hendry smiled faintly, sensing some careful phrasing in Jo's words. "That will do for a start," he accepted.

It was Ted's turn to reveal some confidential information. "Our uncle is being held in remand, but well guarded. He will be coming up for trial in about two months. I don't expect Tom and Jo to be involved in that, though it is a possibility. I fully expect he will be sent to prison for a long stretch."

Scott nodded. He intended to keep aware of the situation.

The meeting ended and Ted decided to treat his siblings to milkshakes and doughnuts as a reward for their improved schoolwork.

Chapter 22

"Sir!"

Ted Dwyer looked around and saw a young girl, dressed in jeans and sweater, just behind him.

"Did you want me?" Ted asked. The girl was younger than his sister.

"The boy over there," she pointed towards where the boats were moored. "He asked me to tell you that he saw two kids being forced on board an old wooden boat that is usually moored over there. He says he's watching it."

Ted scanned the scene, spotted a face he knew and experienced a surge of alarm. An old wooden boat was indeed putting out into the bay.

"Paul! Fred Jackson. Over there!"

Paul Fletcher, Ted's partner, looked up, saw Jackson and took off at a run. He was one of a list of people they were looking out for.

"Did the boy describe these kids?" Ted asked the girl.

"No, he just said kids."

"Thank you, I'll look into it."

The girl watched the man she'd spoken to run over towards a police car and use the radio. The boy had said he was police, even if he was out of uniform. He had been right. When he then raced towards the dock, the girl followed. This was better than watching TV.

Belatedly, she wondered if she should have mentioned the odd bundles she saw being loaded onto that other wooden wreck. The bloke had told her dad it was sail canvas. But it didn't look like that to her! The wooden mast was as rotten as the rest of the boat. She doubted it would support a sail, but that old hulk had motored off an hour ago.

Ted Dwyer reported briefly to the control room — requesting the message be forwarded to Inspector Kent, and for a backup unit to be sent. He was gone before Kent could reply. It sounded like a trap. Dwyer was an exceptional officer, but he had a blind spot where his siblings were concerned.

As Kent tried to get a message back to Ted Dwyer, a messenger gave him a report. Edward Dwyer had escaped. Kent knew that he was due to come up before the judge later that day – but he had not arrived with the group from the prison.

"When did this happen?" Kent demanded.

"It was only just discovered. It could have happened up to two hours ago."

Kent thanked the messenger and went straight out to his car and drove as fast as allowable to the marina at Williamstown. He pulled up next to the car Dwyer and Fletcher were using and the divisional wagon that had arrived to back them up.

"What's happening?" he asked the officers from the van.

"We have Fred Jackson in the van, Sir. Sergeant Fletcher took off after Constable Dwyer. Something about some kids seen forced onto a boat down at the pier."

"Who was the informant?"

"A kid, who claimed Jackson had told her."

Kent strode off in the direction Fletcher had taken and met him returning. He was scanning the boats out on the water.

"Where's Dwyer?" Kent asked Fletcher.

"I can't find him. He might have gone off on one of the boats. Several have just gone out."

"What's this about kids being forced on a boat?"

"No one I have spoken to saw anything, but there is usually an old, rotting clinker boat moored at the jetty. That's missing. One of the men I spoke to saw someone talking to the crew of the 'Sovereign'. He got on board and the boat went out. They were heading in the general direction that the wooden boat had taken."

To the patrol officers, Kent said, "Keep looking around. Find out what you can. Fletcher, take Jackson and have him questioned."

Kent watched his colleagues go off and gave thought to what else he could do.

"Sir!"

Kent turned to see a small girl.

"Are you police?" she asked nervously.

"Yes, I'm Inspector Kent. Do you need to tell me something?"

"I told the blond guy about two kids being forced on a boat. I saw his mate go after the boy who told me to talk to him. I didn't see what he saw, but I did see something I thought odd."

The girl mentioned the odd bundles that had been taken on an old boat earlier. Kent indicated for the girl to walk with him.

"What was the boat you saw the bundles go on?"

"It was an old wooden yacht. Really old. It didn't have a name on it and the paint is almost all flaked off. Dad delivered some bait and ice to it. That's how come I saw the two bundles."

"Kelsey!"

The girl turned around. "That's my Dad."

Kent walked with the girl to the man. "Your daughter was telling me about an old boat you delivered bait and ice to." Kent explained.

"The old one, from the mooring," Kelsey added.

"Oh, that one. They are going to take it to Sandringham and put it on the slip there and work on it. Good thing it's such a calm day, it has only got a small outboard motor and I don't know how seaworthy it is."

"What were the two men like?" Kent asked.

"Nothing special. One was short, wiry. Had dark hair. Italian, probably. The other was taller, solid, with brown hair, balding on top. They both had overalls on. Grey with a red logo."

"The Italian is Spiv and his mate is Moose," Kelsey added, giggling at the silly names.

Kent thanked them for the information. "How can I reach you if I need to ask you anything else?"

The man gave him a business card with his name, Mick King, and a mobile phone number. He seemed glad to be allowed to go on his way.

Kent filed the information in his memory. It didn't seem to relate to the immediate situation. The other wooden boat seemed to be more important, if Ted Dwyer had in fact raced off after it. He walked back to his car and asked to be patched through to the water police. He alerted them to the possibility of trouble.

It nagged at his mind that Ted had hared off, without backup, at about the same time that his uncle had been reported missing. Edward Dwyer couldn't have known where Ted was – could he? Admittedly, Dwyer and Fletcher had been working around the marina for a few days. Perhaps some of Dwyer's mates had seen him there?

"Control, Kent. Can you connect me to my home number?" Kent heard the phone ring and his wife answer.

"Gayle Kent."

"Hello, dear," Kent spoke into his radio transmitter. "Are Tom and Jo there with the twins?"

"No, Will has just gone off to meet them. They were working for the guy at the milk bar until four."

"Give me a call when they are back and keep them there. Their uncle has escaped, but don't worry them just yet."

He heard his wife draw in a deep breath. "Yes, dear, I'll do that."

Kent concluded his radio telephone call. His sense of urgency increased, illogically. What else could he do? Yes! The Jackson boy. He needed to find out what the boy knew and what he was doing at the marina.

Cocky young sot, Kent thought as Jackson smirked and continued to claim innocence of any wrongdoing.

"Why did you get the girl to pass the message," Kent asked in a hard tone.

"I was doing my civic duty. I was watching the boat. She was going that way."

"Why did you run?"

"I didn't want to be blamed for anything. I reported what I saw to the police and I had other things to do."

"What things?"

"Just things! Looking at boats, seeing if I could find work," Jackson claimed.

"How did you get there? You live in Footscray, don't you?"

"I caught a tram and a train and walked the rest of the way," Fred said readily.

"Which train and tram?" Kent quizzed.

Jackson smirked as he gave the tram's route number and train destination. Kent wanted to wipe the smirk from his face.

"Well, it seems that the police officer who heard your tale is missing. Coincidentally, he is the brother of the two children you have a legal order to keep away from. Also, coincidentally, your father is mates with a man who has already tried to kill that officer once already and who escaped from custody today."

"I know nothing about that!" Jackson protested, but the smirk had gone. His old man would kill him if he found out that the police were interested in him because of his son's big mouth.

Kent looked thoughtfully at Jackson. Was he just a little bit frightened? He'd stopped demanding to know why he'd been picked up.

"We're looking at the very least at abduction," Kent said slowly. "The way I see it, you are an accomplice. If that police officer turns up dead, and I fear that is Eddy Dwyer's intention, you will be accessory to murder."

Kent was guessing, based on his worst-case scenario of the afternoon's events. He saw Jackson turn pale and sweaty.

"No, No! They only said he was going to be framed. Put into a compromising position," Jackson blabbed. "He said the kids were only going to get a thrashing."

"Who told you?"

"Dad and the Italian," Jackson blurted. "Honest! They just wanted to discredit the cop. I just had to tell him what they told me and get him to go along the jetty."

Jackson, once he started, told everything he knew, including how he had helped in the abduction of Tom and Jo Dwyer. He described the fish van, one his father often drove. It had dropped him at Williamstown and gone down further to the boats. Kent gestured a constable to pass that news on.

Jackson went on to say that he was to look out for the cop and trick him into going down the jetty. He had been hanging around for about an hour before he'd seen the cop.

Kent left his colleagues to type up the statement and contacted the water police. They now had two boats to look for as well as the fish van.

Shortly after he'd finished with Jackson, his wife rang to say Tom and Jo were missing.

"Ahoy, Sovereign," Ted Dwyer called to the men tidying the charter boat.

"What's up, mate?" one of the hands responded. He left of sluicing the decks of scales and fish blood.

"The boat that was here, the old wooden one, where did it go?" Ted asked the man.

"To the rip to be sunk, I hope," the man joked. "It's an eyesore! Really, though, I don't know. We've just got back."

"I need to find where it's gone," Ted said further. "Are you available to go out again? It's police business."

Ted brought out his ID and showed the man his badge."

"I'll ask the boss, the man agreed, and he climbed nimbly down into the cabin. He returned quickly.

"It's okay with the boss. We've enough fuel still for several hours running. He said that he thinks the owners of that rot trap may have decided to move it round to the jetty. Anyway, hop on, we'll get underway."

Ted watched as the crew efficiently removed the mooring lines and hooked them onto a hook on the piles on each side of the pen. One of them then climbed up to the fly bridge and started the motors, then eased the boat out of its pen. So far, he hadn't seen any sight of the boss.

"I should talk to your skipper about reimbursement for your trouble," Ted offered.

"He'll be up in a while," the crew who had gone back to washing the decks said. "He's cleaning up inside. One of our passengers made quite a mess. Give him ten minutes. Do you want to go round to the jetty first?"

"Yes if you would."

The crewman talked into an intercom and directed the helmsman. Ted scanned the surrounding water as the boat moved slowly amongst the moored boats. He saw nothing of the missing clinker boat.

"It might have gone further up river or out into the bay," Ted was told when the jetty was found to be empty of boats. "Do you want to do a sweep out further?"

"Yes, please. Do you have radar on board?"

"Yes, but it won't be much use. It won't show up a wooden boat and there are too many other boats around that would show up."

Once the boat was out of the mooring area, it increased speed and began a sweep of the area. Ted reasoned that the wooden boat with its slow speed wouldn't have got far. A third crew member appeared on the outer deck.

"Boss, says you can come down now."

Ted climbed down into the cabin, but before his eyes could adjust to the dimness, after the vivid sunshine outside, he was grabbed by both arms.

"What is this?" he demanded.

"This is a one way trip, nephew!"

"Uncle…" Ted recognised the voice.

"So good of you to drop in!"

Edward Dwyer moved forward to examine his erstwhile nephew.

"What have you done with Tom and Jo?" Ted demanded.

"Why nothing," Dwyer said suavely, removing Ted's gun from its shoulder holster. "As you can see, they are not here."

"Where's the wooden boat?"

"Oh, they aren't on that. That was just a decoy. I wouldn't worry. You'll be joining them shortly. I have decided that you have outlasted your usefulness."

"What do you mean?"

"I mean, that you have become as interfering as your old man and those kids are worse. I mean to see that you don't spoil my plans anymore. I'll fix you all like I fixed Ralph Dwyer."

"You killed my father! Your own brother!" Ted knew he wasn't but wanted to hear what the man would say.

"Ralph was not my brother. He was a nuisance, but I fixed him. He had an accident, lost his memory. I convinced him I was his brother and wanted to help him. He worked for me for years. Then the old derelict regained his wits and remembered his wife and kids and became squeamish about working for me. I told him you were all dead. Killed in the accident that lost him his memory – where he had crashed his car into a tree. It destroyed him. He went and walked in front of a train. Saved me the trouble of finishing him off."

"Why did you tell us he was dead?"

"I wanted you all where I could watch you. Just in case Ralph proved even more troublesome. Besides, having you around was useful. Particularly once you became a cop! Who would suspect me of being a crook? Well. That isn't the case anymore. It is time for you and those brats to disappear and for me to make a strategic retreat."

"What are you intending to do?" Ted hoped he'd be fool enough to tell him.

"You don't need to know."

Ted started to struggle, but Dwyer made no move to interfere. The boat slowed to a stop and the helmsman came into the cabin. He fiddled with something he took from a side locker.

Ted hardly felt the jab of the hypodermic needle, but soon felt fuzzy. The men holding him maintained their grip until the policeman finally stopped struggling. Then they dragged him onto a bunk.

"Tie him up," Dwyer ordered. "Take him out to the Euston, then get back to dock. You know what to do then."

When Will and Wendy had gone off with Mrs Kent driving them to where they played basketball, Tom and Jo introduced themselves to the shopkeeper.

"Mike had to play in a basketball match. He asked us to cover for him as he didn't want you going shorthanded," Tom explained.

"He told me you'd be coming. As it happens, I don't have a lot that needs doing. You could help me move some stock from the back storeroom. I'll give you a list of what I need and show you where to look…"

With two of them working, moving stock, sweeping and other general jobs, the work was finished in half the time they expected to be working. The shopkeeper paid them for their time.

Tom and Jo went out of the shop and looked around.

"Not much use waiting around here for Will to come back," Jo decided. "We may as well start walking to the Kent's place."

"Okay. Do you still have a key?"

"In my zip pocket," Jo confirmed. "When we get there, we can give Aunt Gayle a call on her mobile and let her know we are there."

"Sounds good to me," Tom agreed. "It's a nice day for walking."

They kept to the main road and after a while became aware of someone walking behind them.

"What are you up to, Jackson?" Tom demanded. "You have to keep away from us."

"It's a free street – and well – you approached me!"

"You were following us!" Jo accused. "Nick off. You're stinking up the whole street."

Jackson smelt of rotting fish.

"I see you've slipped your baby sitters," Jackson said nastily.

"I can see you need one!" Tom retorted, turning his back on Jackson and walking onwards. Jo copied his attitude.

They were approaching the roadside market that operated on weekends near the park. The stalls all sold fresh produce of some kind, vegetables, fruit, eggs, fish – that sort of thing.

Neither Tom nor Jo paid any attention to the vendor's stalls, and were unprepared for the men who grabbed them from behind, held a hand over their mouths and dragged them into a van smelling of fish. It happened so quickly that they had no chance to use their self-defence skills. As soon as they were released they spun around and pushed on the door, but it had slammed shut and they heard bolts securing the door. They had no way to open it from the inside and very little space amongst they empty racks to move around. They began to kick at the door, but as the truck began to move off and accelerate, they had to hang on to keep their balance. They didn't notice, amongst the strong smell of fish, the anaesthetic gas seeping into the back of the truck. They were too busy trying to attract attention by kicking the door and keeping warm as the refrigeration unit chilled the air.

Will arrived at the shop at four o'clock and looked around. Seeing no sign of his friends, he went into the shop and asked for them.

"Are Tom and Jo around?"

"They went off about three," The man told Will. "Very hard workers, that pair. Mike picked well."

"Damn," Will surprised the shopkeeper, "Did they say where they were going?"

"Not that I heard. What's the matter?"

"No matter – they've probably walked home. I was meant to meet them here, that's all. Thanks."

Will trotted off towards his house – sure they would be waiting there. At least they had a key to get in. When he arrived home, he was prepared to give Tom a few choice words.

"Where are they," Wendy greeted his return.

"They left an hour ago. Aren't they here?"

"No," Wendy went pale. "Mum! Mum!"

"I'm sure it's nothing," Gayle Kent said calmly – feeling far from it. "They may have lost their way or stopped for a rest. I'll let your father know. He can have people look out for them if he feels it is necessary."

Wendy listened to her mother's calm tone as she spoke to her father on the phone. She was beginning to feel that her first panicked reaction was silly. Then she heard the news bulletin on the radio and heard that Edward Dwyer had escaped. She almost became physically sick with worry.

Tom and Jo had just begun to relax. Today was the first day they had ventured out on their own in the four months since their uncle had been arrested – even though with him in custody they hadn't needed to fear him. They had finally settled down at school and stopped playing tricks. They were working so hard to make up for being unable to study and complete assignments at home. They had finally got over their fear of their uncle's threat – now this. It wasn't fair!

Wendy hoped, desperately, that they would hurry up and walk in the door. It occurred to her to ring Kath Daniels – in case they had gone there, but they hadn't.

Chapter 23

The marina swarmed with police. Boat owners were questioned. Some had noticed Ted Dwyer, but none had spoken to him. The crew of the charter boat Sovereign made no mention of Dwyer being on board or having spoken to them. They admitted to going out, because they had needed to refuel and they admitted noticing the old clinker boat had gone. They didn't know where.

The wooden boat mentioned by twelve-year-old Kelsey King had not returned either and had not arrived at Sandringham. Her observations had suddenly taken on major importance.

By five o'clock, three police boats, the police helicopter and seven coast guard patrol boats were actively looking for the two wooden boats. There would only be an hour or two of daylight left, after which the helicopter would have to land. The Coast Guard boats were checking their assigned areas, though once it was dark most would be returning to their bases.

One of the police boats was patrolling up the Yarra River and the Maribyrnong River and around the docks. They realised that Eddy Dwyer, who worked at the docks, might have known of places where an unwanted cargo could be off loaded.

The old yacht, for so long a neglected, rotting hulk, had looked grey brown. After motoring slowly out into the bay, the two crew had unrolled a bolt of white calico and nailed it to the sloping upper deck, and also removed the mast. From air and sea, it now looked a completely different vessel.

There was another factor that wasn't obvious. The small motor that had powered it away from the dock was not its only power source. It also had a carefully overhauled inboard motor, giving it an actual top speed of seven knots, not the two knots of the little auxiliary motor. So by the time a search was instigated, it had travelled much further than anyone would have guessed possible and was well out of the search area. The two men on board at the time it left the marina had told people they were heading for Sandringham, but in fact, they had headed due south towards The Rip.

Just on dusk, the police found the clinker boat tied up at an unused jetty near the docks. The boat was deserted, but the police found on board two pairs of sport shoes, too small for the men who had last been seen in the boat, a few links of chain and traces of hessian sacking. That section of the docks was immediately sealed off and an intensive search began both on shore and with divers searching the murky water nearby. Two lighting trucks were moved into place to illuminate the water.

Inspector Kent sat in the police boat, VP10 and listened to the marine traffic on the radios. He soon tuned out to the traffic on the 27MHz radio band and concentrated on the VHF radio frequencies. There was little of importance to be heard, except the report from the Coast Guard radio base station reporting the return of four of the patrol boats to base. Though he felt helpless, he appreciated the willingness of the Coast Guard volunteers to help in the search.

"Hey, Andy," Kelly Phillips called to his cousin. "Is that a boat over there without lights on?"

The two were fishing, and it was almost midnight. Andy Phillips looked where Kelly was pointing.

"Reckon so. Where are we?"

As they had been letting their boat drift, Kelly went into the cabin and turned on the GPS. "We're close to the shipping channel. We'd better move."

Andy pulled in his fishing line and stowed it. Kelly did the same.

"Start the motor, Kel," Andy told him. "We'll do a run around that boat. Tell the people on it to move out of the channel and put lights on."

Kelly was perfectly at home on the Porpoise and motored slowly over to the other drifting boat.

"Ahoy!" Andy called loudly. There was no answer. "Closer, Kel. Nudge up to it."

Kelly felt the bump as the bow of the Porpoise touched the other boat. Andy leant over the side of his boat and rapped on the upper deck of the other boat.

"Ahoy! Anyone on board? You are drifting into the shipping channel and your lights are off." Andy had a torch shining on the other boat. There was still no answer.

"What now?" Kelly asked. "Do we tow it?"

"I'll call the Coast Guard, they can deal with it," Andy decided. He moved down into the cabin to where the radio was switched on.

"Coast Guard, Coast Guard, this is Porpoise, Porpoise, on VHF channel 16, Over."

"Porpoise, this is Coast Guard Melbourne. Change to Channel 67, Over."

"Changing up," Andy acknowledged.

"Coast Guard to Porpoise, go ahead. Over."

"Coast Guard, we have found a boat drifting close to the shipping channel, about five miles south of the Fawkner Beacon. It appears deserted and has no lights on. Should we tow it in? Over."

"Porpoise, can you give us a description of the vessel and its registration number? Over."

"It's a wooden boat, displacement hull, about twenty foot long and a curved upper deck. We've been right around it with a torch and we can't find a registration number. There might have been one but the paint is flaking off all over the hull. Over."

"How close to the channel is the vessel? Over."

"Less than a quarter of a mile. I can give you our GPS position, over."

"Go ahead, Porpoise. Over."

Andy read his position off the GPS and the Coast Guard radio operator read back the latitude and longitude figures to confirm them.

"Stand by the vessel, Porpoise. We'll have a vessel out to you as soon as possible. If the vessel drifts into the channel, you may have to tow it, but stay clear otherwise. Could we have a description of your vessel, please? Over."

Andy described his twenty-two foot cabin cruiser and gave its registration number. He added that there were only two of them on board.

"Thank you, Porpoise. We will be listening out on channel 16 if you need to call us again. Out."

"Porpoise, Out.'

"A little bit of excitement," Kelly commented. "How long do you reckon it will take the Coast Guard to get here?"

"Depends on where they have to come from and how long it takes them to get a crew back," Andy mused, sniffing the air. "They are only volunteers. Most of the bases close down at dark."

"Well, we don't have to worry about the Spirit of Tasmania coming down on us," Kelly remarked. "She's gone past already."

"At least you can see her coming from miles off. She's lit up like a Christmas tree. It's some of the container boats you have to watch out for. Sometimes you can't see them until they are almost on top of you!" Andy told his cousin.

"Radar might be useful right now," Kelly replied wryly.

"Can you smell a smoky smell?" Andy asked suddenly.

"Vaguely," Kelly decided. "There was a lot of smoke from burning off today. Could we be smelling that? The breeze is off-shore now."

"It could be that," Andy considered. "Though, it doesn't smell like grass fire smoke. It seems oilier."

Andy took over the wheel and circled the dark drifting boat.

"I can't see anything wrong," Andy had to admit. He moved a little away and turned off the motor. The cousins settled down to wait.

"You weren't long getting here!" Andy greeted the Coast Guard crew as the patrol boat idled close to his boat.

"We were still on the water. We had just finished towing a boat into Sandringham, so we were asked to respond. What have you got?"

"Some old boat, drifting with no lights." Andy's tone indicated his disgust.

"Good thing you spotted it. Any sign of passengers?"

"No, none at all," Andy reported.

The Coast Guard crew member turned to his colleague behind the wheel.

"Put the spot light on it, Jim, and nudge in so that I can get aboard. Then get the tow line ready."

Kelly was fascinated by the effortless ease with which the crewman crossed to the drifting boat. The coast Guard vessel, CG07, had idled to touch the other boat with the merest of pressure.

"Nothing on it to tie a rope to," was the comment from the crewman on the drifting boat. "Might have to tie the line to the mast step. Even that doesn't look too strong. Can you pass a torch across, Jim? I'd better check below."

CG07 moved to be side on to the other vessel and the torch was passed across.

"Be careful down there, Wayne," the crewman on CG07 warned his mate. Wayne grinned and walked carefully to the cockpit and flashed the torch inside. His first sweep showed only a bundle of something forward before he checked the mounting of the mast step.

"It reeks of smoke down here," Wayne told Jim. "The inside is completely stripped, right down to the outer hull. There's lots of water in the bilge, too. There's a bundle of some kind in the bow. You'd better give Coast Guard Melbourne a call and tell them what we've found. Find out if the police want it towed anywhere. This might be one of the boats they had us looking for earlier."

Kelly and Andy could hear Jim talking on the radio and being answered, but the conversation wasn't on channel 16 or 67.

Wayne had disappeared down into the drifting boat. A muffled exclamation drew everyone's attention to the drifting boat. A few minutes later, Wayne appeared, looking very grim. He glanced at the two men on the cabin cruiser.

"Would one of you be able to come aboard and give me a hand?"

"Ok," Kelly volunteered at once. Andy attempted to copy the manoeuvre of the Coast Guard boat.

"Just pull alongside" Wayne suggested. "I'll hold your boat there long enough for one of you to scramble over. Then you'd best move away. Something is smouldering in here."

"They want to know if we found anyone on board," Jim called to Wayne.

"Yes," Wayne confirmed. "Tell them there are three people on board and request the police to meet us and have an ambulance standing by."

Jim didn't waste time with questions. He returned to the radio and passed on the information and was back on deck as Kelly and Wayne were lifting out a wrapped bundle from the drifting ship.

Jim manoeuvred CG07 alongside the other boat and quickly tied the gunnels together. Kelly rested the end of the bundle he was carrying on the gunnels and Wayne held what he guessed was the head of a young woman as Jim lifted her legs further onto CG07. Kelly then hopped over to CG07 and supported the head until Wayne hopped over himself. The Coast Guard crew carried the unconscious woman into the cabin and rested her on the cushions in there.

Wayne and Kelly wasted no time in returning to the other boat. Jim checked the woman, found a pulse, and noted she was breathing shallowly. He came back outside and helped with the second blanket wrapped bundle. This one reeked of smoke and was soaked through. The procedure was the same.

"I know these kids," Kelly said as he got a good look at the second bundle.

"Perhaps you would stay with them for a moment," Wayne asked as he returned yet again to the other boat.

Wayne went up to the bow and helped the third person he'd found to stagger to his feet. He had earlier used his very sharp pocketknife to cut off ropes binding the man and while he had been helping the other two, this man's brother and sister, the man had ripped off the tape from his mouth and begun to massage his wrists and ankles to restore circulation to his limbs.

"Don't try to talk," Wayne told the man. "We have coffee and water on CG07 and we really should get off this boat as soon as we can. It seems to be sinking and something seems to be smouldering."

Ted Dwyer managed, with help, to stagger up into the cockpit of the derelict. He crossed awkwardly and with help, to the Coast Guard boat. Jim helped him to the navigator's chair and then went to pass the towline to Wayne. They worked together like a well-drilled team. Wayne secured one end of the line and Jim played out line from a reel secured in the workspace. When Wayne had returned to his own boat, he untied the rope joining the two boats and played out the towline as Jim moved CG07 forward.

"Good thing the sea is flat calm," Wayne remarked to Jim. "I'd hate to have to tow this thing in any kind of sea."

Wayne held onto the towline and beckoned the cruiser back over.

"Kelly," Jim called into the cabin. "Are you ready to go back to your own boat?"

"Right," Kelly appeared. "Will the police need us?"

"They might," Wayne warned. "VP10 is coming down to meet us. They shouldn't be much longer getting here. You said you knew the kids?"

"Yeah, they go to my school."

"We're to head towards Williamstown, where they will have an ambulance waiting. It would probably be a good idea if you follow us in, in case the police want to ask you about finding the boat."

Kelly crossed back to his cousin's boat and began telling his cousin what was going on.

Wayne began letting more towline out once the Porpoise had moved away.

"I'm going to let most of the line out," Wayne told Jim. "If this hulk begins to burn, not just smoulder, I don't want to be too close. Though it might sink before it burns. It's going to be awful to tow."

"Good practice," Jim shrugged. "Coast Guard wants a report."

Wayne went into the cabin and checked on the condition of the other two rescued victims. The third man was sitting there with them. He had a drink of water in his hand.

"They are breathing okay. Do you have any blankets to put around them instead of the wet ones?" Ted Dwyer spoke in a strained voice.

Wayne pulled out two blankets from a locker under one of the cushions. He passed one to Ted and wrapped one around the girl who was nearest him. It was then that he realised that the girl was tied up as the man had been, but without the tape on the mouth.

He took out his pocket knife once again.

"That's a dangerous little item," Ted managed to say. "Useful, though."

"Isn't it?" Wayne said neutrally. "Particularly when we need to cut a tow line in a hurry or get into strife."

He cut the ropes binding the girl's wrists and ankles and passed the knife to the other man to do the same for the boy.

"I appreciate your help," Ted told Wayne. He felt in his pockets and was relieved to feel his ID wallet. He pulled it out and fumbled it open. The badge was identifiable and the card had been laminated and had survived the immersion in the water in the bilge of the derelict boat.

"Do you want us to tell the water police you are here?" Wayne asked.

Ted shook his head. "I don't want just anyone to hear it?"

"We could tell Coast Guard Melbourne, on our domestic frequency and they can contact the police by landline."

"You said VP10 would be here soon," Ted recalled. "I'll talk to them then. What time is it?"

"Nearly one o'clock."

It seemed that Ted Dwyer was calculating something.

"You could pass something on for me," Ted decided. "I went out on a boat called Sovereign, one of the charter boats. That's where I was knocked out. I came to for a bit when they were transferring me to that hulk. I saw another boat, it was a Caribbean, about 35 foot, with a fly bridge. I think the name on it was Ruby Sunset, MC507V. They need to watch out for it."

CG07 began to pick up speed, to keep the tow from fishtailing too wildly. Wayne watched the tow from the cabin.

"I'll pass on the details. Do you want to wait in here?"

"I'd rather be above," Ted opted. He wanted the chance to look out for his uncle.

Wayne accepted his choice without comment and continued to watch the tow, even as he called his base on the radio and logged the call. Suddenly he said, "Whoa, Jim, slow down. That boat back there is beginning to glow."

CG07 slowed right down and Wayne pulled in some of the towline, gradually letting it out again as CG07 continued forward at the slower speed. The glow faded as the wind caused by its speed decreased. Ted was staring at the derelict.

"I can't thank you enough for getting us off there," Ted said sincerely.

"You're welcome, mate. It's what we're around for. Though it was a good thing the other blokes spotted the boat drifting in the dark and called us. Too many boaties would have cursed the boat and gone on their way."

"Could you thank them?"

"They are following us to Williamstown," Wayne told Ted. "We still need to get some details from them for our paperwork."

"You might have to write an account of finding us too," Ted warned.

"Too bad my secretary is at home with the kids. She writes better than me."

Ted smiled and sat back in the navigator's chair. He heard VP10 calling CG07 and asking for their position. Jim read it off the GPS and VP10 gave their ETA as five minutes.

Ted noticed that the Coast Guard volunteers were quite at ease in the company of the police crew. As the two vessels drifted next to each other, the crews exchanged information and CG07 gained an extra passenger.

"Dwyer," Kent greeted.

"Sir," Ted responded.

"What else can you tell us?"

"Uncle was on one of the hire boats. I went on board because they had agreed to take a quick cruise out to look for the wooden boat this girl mentioned."

Kent nodded.

"One of the crew jabbed me with something and it knocked me out. Next thing I'm aware of is being transferred to that boat," Ted pointed to the vessel being towed. "It wasn't the Sovereign then, but the Ruby Sunset and I heard some talk about heading out to Bass Strait to meet another boat."

"He's probably long gone," Kent sighed.

"I don't necessarily think so," Ted argued weakly. "He intended to get rid of us. I think he would hang around, to be sure. He's arrogant enough."

CG07 began to move again, faster than before.

Jim went into the cabin to check on the two younger passengers, and Ted realised that the wooden boat was now being towed by the police boat. The exchange had been so efficiently managed that he hadn't noticed it.

"Hang on," Wayne warned. He was behind the wheel now and Kent turned to him.

"Did you notice any 35 foot Carribean vessels with a fly bridge, on your way here?"

"There are a lot of big boats out tonight," Wayne commented. "We passed one about half a mile back, before we reached Andy's boat. They had lights on and fishing lines off the back."

"Any that seemed to be taking an interest in what you were doing?"

"I didn't notice any," Wayne admitted. He flicked a switch and turned on the radar.

Kent stood to look at it.

"Were the dot at the centre," Wayne remarked. "There's Andy's boat, keeping up with us and VP10. You can't see the towed boat." Kent watched the line on the screen sweep around.

"What about these two boats. They seem to be keeping up with us."

"They might just be heading back into Williamstown, like us."

There was logic in that. Kent brooded in silence.

"We've got company! VP09," Wayne commented dryly.

"Can you put me aboard her?" Kent requested.

"Sure," Wayne agreed, slowing and putting a radio call into the police boat.

After the exchange of call signs, Wayne said, "We have a passenger who wishes to come aboard. We're coming around to you."

Wayne took CG07 around behind the towed boat and noticed in passing that the vessel was lower in the water than it had been before.

The police had it on a shorter towline than he'd had.

Kent was able to transfer to the police boat without trouble. He turned in time to forestall Ted from following.

"Stay with your brother and sister, Dwyer. That's an order! You are not fit for duty."

Ted sat back with relief.

VP09 began to move off at once, in the direction of the vessels Kent had noticed to be following the Coast Guard boat. VP10 continued to tow the wooden wreck, and CG07 began to move faster, towards Williamstown and the waiting ambulance.

"The two kids are stirring," Jim called from the cabin and Ted went in at once and sat beside Jo and spoke softly to her.

"Your brother and sister, are they?" Jim asked casually.

Ted nodded, relieved when the other man refrained from prying questions.

"We should be tied up at the jetty in 15 to 20 minutes," Jim offered instead.

<h1 align="center">Chapter 24</h1>

"Come on, Jo," Kelly Phillips encouraged. "I know you can hear me. Open your eyes."

"I'm too tired," was the mumbled answer.

"No you're not! You've been sleeping for two days. You need to wake up and have some water."

"Go away Kelly Phillips," Jo tried to insist. "Where's my brother?"

"Two doors down and across the corridor," Kelly told her. He was relieved she had recognised his voice.

"How is he?"

"If you want to know, you'll have to walk down and find out!" Kelly told her. He knew Tom was in the same condition as Jo was.

The doctors saw no reason why the two Dwyers should still be asleep. Post trauma depression perhaps. It seemed likely. Kelly had offered to chivvy Jo, whilst Ted was doing the same to Tom.

"Do you want some water," Kelly asked. He was sitting on a chair next to the bed.

"Yeah, I do," Jo realised. Her mouth was dry and her throat painful. She sipped through the straw that Kelly Phillips put to her lips.

"Slowly!" he cautioned. "Taste each drop."

Jo slumped back onto her pillow. Just that small action exhausted her.

"What hit us? I remember that foul smelling fish van."

"It's a long story. It will keep until you are properly awake."

"My eyes feel like they have glue on them," Jo complained.

Kelly stood up and went to the small en-suite of the ward. He found a face washer and wet it at the tap. The washer was one of the things that Kath Daniels, the friend of Ted Dwyer had packed when she heard that Tom and Jo would be in hospital for a few days.

"Here's a face washer," Kelly said awkwardly. He put it into Jo's hand and wondered if she would use it.

Eventually, Jo began to wash her face and seemed to be enjoying the feel of it.

"All right, tell me. I'll stay awake."

Kelly began his narrative at the time when he and his cousin had found the drifting boat and went on with the story in the order he had learnt it.

"Is Ted all right?" was Jo's first words when Kelly finished speaking.

"Better than you. He was sent home, not kept in here."

"Have they caught Uncle?"

Kelly chuckled maliciously. "You bet! He was so damn sure of himself that he stuck around, waiting to be sure that his plan to rid the world of you had worked. When the Coast Guard and the police found the boat, he didn't dare come close, but he still thought the boat would blow up and burn. But the fuse only smouldered and didn't ignite the fuel tank. He didn't realise that Ted had seen the boat he'd transferred to and heard some of his intentions. While the Coast Guard took you and your brothers to shore, the police went off and found the boat."

"What's to say he won't escape again?" Jo asked.

"He's in more secure custody now, charged with attempted murder. I don't think he'll have a chance."

Jo looked more animated but still lay slumped as if she had no energy.

"I never thought you'd let him get the better of you, Jo," Kelly mused aloud. "You never have before. He's not worth thinking about."

"It's not that easy!" Jo argued weakly.

"Probably not, but I reckon that the best way to put this behind you is to figuratively spit in his eye and get on with your life," Kelly advised.

"You know, he's not really related to us. Ted found out for sure."

"Then you owe him nothing at all," Kelly said flatly. "Come on, I'll help you walk down to see your brother."

Ted was having less effect than Kelly in making Tom wake up and start taking notice of things. He had been greatly relieved when young Phillips had turned up at the hospital and offered to sit with Jo. He had been trying and wanting to be in two places at once.

"Damn it, Tom," Ted swore, betraying his worry and frustration. "It wasn't just you and Jo, he got me again too. I should have been more careful. The bastard had me figured out perfectly. And I couldn't do a damn thing to help you until the coast guard blokes and that kid from your school helped us."

"Who?" Tom decided to ask. "Jackson?"

"No, Kelly Phillips. He and his cousin were out fishing and found the boat we had been dumped in." Ted was glad to have had a response at last.

Tom finally opened his eyes. "Jackson helped them get us."

"We know," Ted told him with a grim smile. "He thought that Uncle was only intending to have us roughed up – seriously roughed up but still alive. When he realised that he might be involved in a murder, he had a rapid change of heart. He couldn't rat on his old man and his other mates fast enough. The upside is, many more of uncle's mates have been arrested and are being questioned in jail."

Tom forced a smile.

"Now, it's time you had some water."

Tom found he really needed the drink and sipped until his glass was empty.

"So how did he get you?" Tom asked sourly.

"Because I was a damn fool," Ted began and he told Tom what had happened.

Tom made no comment. He knew why Ted had acted as he had. They were Dwyers, they stuck together.

"And I've had an almighty bawling out from my superiors," Ted admitted wryly. He caught Tom's eye and they shared a moment of amusement.

"Seems none of us are perfect," Jo spoke from the doorway. Her look passed from Tom to her red-faced eldest brother. "Now I know where we get it from! Hello Tom. Get out of bed you lazy lunk. I had to."

"What! In this dreadful gown thing?" Tom objected.

"Look in your drawer, bro, you might find something better," Jo suggested. "Want me to leave?"

"Yeah, just for a mo'," Tom blushed.

Chapter 25

Ted Dwyer no longer felt the paper clutched in his hand. His mind was recalling, vividly, scenes from his childhood.

"Dad, my hand hurts," he heard himself say in memory.

"Give it here. Son," his father's voice was loving and gentle. He could almost feel the big hands massaging his own.

"Where's mum?"

"In our room, resting. Let her try to sleep."

"What's up?"

"The baby is coming early," his dad told him.

"Where's Tom?"

"Sleeping."

Ted remembered the first time he heard Jo cry. His father had hugged him with a happy smile on his face.

Later, he'd been allowed to see his new sister.

"We've called her Josephine, after my mother," his mum had said.

"She's beautiful, Mum."

His mind flashed through the years as his brother and sister grew.

Then he remembered the night when his father had woken him up in the middle of the night.

"What's up, Dad?"

"I have to leave on a trip. I haven't a choice. I'll come back, as soon as I can. I promise. Look after your mum and your brother and sister for me."

"I will, dad, but why must you go? Why now, in the night?"

"It's important, son. That's all I can say."

Ted recalled hugging his father, trying to stop him leaving. In the morning, he was gone.

Less than a year later, Edward Dwyer, an uncle he'd said, had come to tell him that his father was dead.

Tom and Jo pranced into Kath Daniels house. They were extremely pleased with themselves because they had their end of year results and they had passed well in all subjects.

"We're home," Jo announced loudly. She expected Ted to be there because he had come off night shift that morning. "Ted?"

"I'm here," Ted called from the lounge. He shook his head to clear the memories.

"What's up, Ted? You look awful," Jo asked.

"Yeah, bro, you look like hell!" Tom confirmed.

Sensing that their brother needed them, Tom and Jo dumped their bags and sat on the floor, on either side of his chair.

"What's the letter," Jo asked and Ted let her take it from his hand.

"Jack Grant forwarded it to me, with a package," Ted's voice was husky, as if he was trying not to cry.

Jo read the letter aloud.

"My dear wife Adele, my children, Ted, Tom and Jo.

I am writing this to let you know that I am coming home. These last few years, my life hasn't been my own. Until two days ago, I had no memory of my home, family or work. Because of an accident, I had forgotten everything.

Suddenly, the man I thought was my brother has become a stranger. Familiar, because I have been working for him, but a stranger.

Worse, I have realised that I have been helping to commit crimes for a man I swore to catch and put in jail.

I am so confused. I need my family right now, to help me sort out who I am.

I will be home soon,

Your loving husband, your loving father, Ralph Dwyer."

"Read the date," Ted said.

"December … that's six years ago!" Jo exclaimed. "Then when that bastard brought us to Melbourne, our father wasn't dead!"

"Why would he do that?" Tom said confused. "Do you think our dad might still be alive?"

"No," Ted managed to get out. "When we were visiting the Grant's, Jack told me that he had spoken to a man, who looked like a hobo…"

Ted told his siblings of the conversation.

"Why didn't you tell us?" Tom asked plaintively.

"Because Jack said that… that two days later – a hobo walked in front of a train and was killed."

"It might have been someone else," Jo said with tears streaming from her eyes.

"No, uncle bragged about it," Ted told her. "When he'd lured me onto that boat…"

Ted related that conversation.

"Did you try to find out more about the hobo?" Jo asked.

Ted nodded. "The body was so badly mangled that it had to be identified from the clothes. Uncle identified him but the clothing listed in the report matched what Jack had seen on the man he spoke to. They tried to confirm it from army records but the dead man had no teeth left and no denture work was found. Fingerprints couldn't be obtained and the man was an alcoholic."

Jo hugged Ted's knees and felt his arm around her. Tom stood up and walked away a bit.

"That's not the end of it," Tom said flatly.

"Tom…" Ted began.

"No, let me think this out," Tom insisted. "I was what – four – when father left?"

Ted nodded.

"I'm almost sixteen now – that's twelve years. I started school here, so about eleven years ago 'uncle' turns up and tells Mum and everyone that Dad is dead and then drags us here – out of the goodness of his rotten heart. Five years later, a man wanders into town and he might be our father. By then, Mum is dead and everyone in Tamboora has heard we all died in a car crash. So, that is what the poor man is told. He quizzes his so-called brother, and is told it's true and he was the driver at fault. So the poor man, who is no doubt confused, in shock (if it was our father and the letter is correct) – goes and gets some possessions from somewhere, sends them to Jack to look after until he comes for them and goes and walks in front of a train? If he wanted to kill himself, why bother to get the stuff and why say he'd be back for it?"

"Uncle identified the body," Ted interrupted.

"How?" Tom rebutted. "Army records couldn't identify him. So all we have are the claims of a lying bastard. A man who lied to everyone. It sounds like he hated father and I know he's never liked us. He's probably still laughing at the anguish he's caused all of us."

"What if he's still wandering around somewhere?" Jo looked at Ted. "What if he's convinced we are all dead, convinced he has no one? There's a chance…"

"What did the man give Mr Grant?" Tom interrupted before Ted could squash Jo's idea.

The box was beside Ted – still paper wrapped and sealed and tied with string.

On the paper, written in dark ink, were the words "To be kept for Ralph Dwyer, until I come for it."

"Open it, Ted," Jo told him and she said nothing of the trembling fingers that began to remove the string.

The paper fell open at last to reveal a number of documents and a plastic identification wallet.

Tom and Jo looked through the papers and recognised that they were birth certificates for Ralph and Adele, Ted and themselves as well as their parents wedding certificate. There was also a letter from a solicitor confirming receipt of a wills made by Ralph and Adele.

Ted took the identification wallet and stared into it. Tom and Jo moved to see it.

"He was a policeman too," Tom said amazed. "I thought Jack Grant said he was a salesman?"

"A federal policeman," Ted corrected. "Mum must have known. Why didn't I know?"

"Maybe you blocked it out?" Jo suggested.

"No, I remember him saying he was a representative," Ted recalled. "I don't think I ever knew what for, but he travelled a lot and had to speak to lots of people."

"Maybe you did know," Tom offered. "Maybe that's why you chose to be a policeman. To be like him."

"Ted, can you contact the federal police and see if they know anything about him?" Jo suggested.

"If his badge was in the parcel – he probably didn't report back to them. If he was going to kill himself – he wouldn't."

"Ted – you don't know that," Jo insisted. "If he didn't want to be identified, why not include his driver's licence too? It wasn't found on the body – or that would have confirmed the ID."

"But why hide his badge," Ted asked, almost to himself.

"This is all confusing," Jo admitted. "But in the letter he said he was confused. He'd committed crimes – perhaps he needed time to sort himself out. Personally first, and then come back and sort out his professional life. He'd need his driver's licence to get around."

"But uncle identified the body…" Ted insisted.

"Stop calling him uncle," Tom shouted, then he moderated his voice. "The bastard could have been wrong! He thought he was going to kill us and get clean away! He was wrong there! Anyway, how's this for an idea? Father has had amnesia but suddenly recalls all of us. Ok, he's confused and he might have been drinking a lot in those years. He travels to Tamboora, possibly on foot and since he's escaping from you know who he might be dirty and looking like a hobo. He hears we are dead and that's a shock to him, but he goes and gets his private papers and sends them to his old friend instead. That suggests planning. He's recalled his so-called brother is a crook and decides to do something about it, so he first goes and cleans himself up and gets new clothes. Perhaps he gives the old clothes to the first homeless deadbeat he sees. Perhaps uncle could only identify the clothes – perhaps he really thinks Ralph Dwyer is dead."

"You are clutching at straws," Ted told him. "He's not likely to be still alive."

"Can't we look some more," Jo pleaded. "Please?"

"I never thought you'd feel so strongly," Ted was seeing his siblings in a new light. They didn't seem like children any more.

"I agree with Jo, Ted. I meant what I said the other day. I haven't missed having a father. I knew I always had you. But if there is a Dwyer out there somewhere – who is really one of us – as you said – we've got to stick together."

Tom and Jo hugged their older brother and ignored the tears he was spilling.

"We'll do it!" Ted finally agreed. "We'll look for him. Don't get your hopes too high though. Once Uncle's trial is over…"

"Don't call him Uncle!" Tom repeated.

The reminder of the trial depressed them all. Each of them had appeared in court, testifying to aspects of Eddy Dwyer's crimes. It was an ordeal indeed with the venomous eyes of their supposed uncle on them. The trial itself kept being suspended as new evidence came to light and was further complicated by the trials of his cohorts.

"Whenever that will be," Jo sniffed.

"What with all those high priced lawyers delaying all the time," Tom added.

"Anyway," Jo changed the subject "I don't want to think about that. Tom and I have something to show you and I think it will be good enough to get us a meal at Macca's."

Ted wiped his eyes and released his siblings. They each went to their school bag and pulled out a white envelope.

"Here," Jo pushed the paper from the envelope into his hands.

"Here,' Tom pushed his result sheet at his brother too.

Ted's face developed a proud smile.

"Yes, I think a reward is definitely in order. Macca's today and when uncle is sent away we will all go to the swankest restaurant I can find."

"Mmm, I can't wait," Jo hugged her brother again. "Your shout of course," she added cheekily.

Chapter 26

The last day of school dawned. Tom and Jo were up as the sun rose, full of excitement. Yesterday, glorious yesterday, Edward Dwyer or Edward Dixon as he was originally named, was sentenced to thirty years in prison.

"If I don't do something today, I'll burst," Tom told his sister at breakfast.

"I know the feeling," Jo agreed. "And I only agreed to behave until today. Now today has come … are you game?"

Tom nodded and waited as Jo dived into her bedroom and returned with a medium sized box.

"Trick chalk, trick duster, the hand that gets stuck in the door, fake sick, fake ink blots, giggle cushion, whoopee cushion…what do you want?"

Fortunately, Ted wasn't home from duty yet or he might have been concerned by the giggles emanating from the kitchen. Kath Daniels heard them, but they sounded so happy that she said nothing.

Kelly Phillips was walking with Marc Hendry and they could hear the howls of laughter coming from the Ten Silver classroom.

"I hope they are not starting up again," Hendry sighed. He was glad the year was all but over.

Kelly knew exactly whom 'they' referred to. He had caught Jo putting inkblots on his letter of recommendation from the school. Fortunately, they had peeled off.

"I don't think so, Sir," Kelly reassured him. "You've seen how they've improved. I'm sure it's just high spirits today. After all, their uncle was finally sentenced yesterday. And even though I was one of their victims this morning – I'm relieved to see them like this. They were depressed for a long while after their abduction. It's good to see how they have bounced back."

"Put like that, I would have to agree," Hendy admitted. "But next year…"

"Is another year," Kelly grinned.

The End

he can coerce through fear. Erin was perfect.
SHORT STORIES:

GRAFFITI GIRL
Valerie has become known as "The Graffiti Girl" but she is more
than just a street artist.
She sees and paints life her way.

In Valkyrie, the second story, Valerie, blinded by an explosion,
must learn to paint and see again.

GHOST WRITER
Edwina is a ghost with a mission - to find out why she died.
Only to do so, she must first help another girl.